From behind, a hand clamped her shoulder.

Her heart ricocheted. Casey jerked around to see a man with piercing blue eyes staring back. Though the look on his face was anything but friendly, relief swept through her. This man didn't have the look of a crazed killer. She should know. For a fleeting moment, she had feared Will Tannin had caught up with her. Her breathing slowed, if only a little.

"What are you doing here?" he asked.

Taken aback at his guarded tone, Casey struggled for words, something that didn't happen often to her as a journalist.

"You shouldn't be here. Let's go." He glanced over her shoulder at something behind her, a sense of urgency in his eyes, and grabbed her arm. "The loading dock is off-limits. It isn't safe. You could get hurt."

Casey sensed that this story had just got a lot more interesting.

ELIZABETH GODDARD

is a seventh-generation Texan who grew up in a small oil town in East Texas, surrounded by Christian family and friends. Becoming a writer of Christian fiction was a natural outcome of her love of reading, fueled by a strong faith.

Elizabeth attended the University of North Texas where she received her degree in computer science. She spent the next seven years working in high-level sales for a software company located in Dallas, and traveling throughout the United States and Canada as part of the job. At twenty-five, she finally met the man of her dreams and married him a few short weeks later. When she had her first child, she moved back to East Texas with her husband and daughter and worked for a pharmaceutical company. But then, more children came along and it was time to focus on family. Elizabeth loves that she gets to do her favorite things every day—read, write novels, stay at home with her four precious children, and work with her adoring husband in ministry.

FREEZING POINT

Elizabeth Goddard

Love Inspired

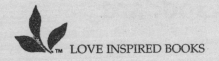 LOVE INSPIRED BOOKS

Recycling programs
for this product may
not exist in your area.

ISBN-13: 978-0-373-67484-8

FREEZING POINT

www.LoveInspiredBooks.com

Printed in U.S.A.

I will say of the Lord, He is my refuge and my fortress; My God, in Him will I trust.
—*Psalms* 91:2

As always, my stories are dedicated to
my loving husband and my four beautiful children.

Acknowledgments

I couldn't have written this without help from
Mindi Smith, a twenty-year veteran with the FBI.
Thanks, Mindi, for your invaluable assistance
and sticking with me on this project.
Thanks to Ken Ackerman of Dryiceinfo.com
for explaining how to make dry ice work
for my story, and to Dale Pierce of Creative Ice
for answering questions about ice sculpting.
To my critique partners (you know who you are),
and to Ellen Tarver, thank you for making my
stories shine. A special thank you to my agent,
Steve Laube, for believing in me, and to my editor,
Emily Rodmell, for believing in this story!

ONE

Beautiful...but dangerous.

Jesse finished shoving the last block of dry ice into the back of the specially designed truck—well insulated, yet ventilated to allow for sublimation — the melting that would give off deadly CO_2 gas.

The solid form of carbon dioxide would be used to create the snow effect around the ice sculptures along with fog—a mysterious yet stunning display.

He tugged off the gloves used to protect his hands from ice burns or, worse, frostbite. Because his father was a chef and master ice sculptor, Jesse had learned a few techniques of his own, even entering competitions during his college days.

That's what made him the perfect candidate for this covert operation, and the only reason Robert McCoffey, his superior, had pulled Jesse from the desk job and visits to the psychiatrist and put him back into the action. Working as an undercover agent for Immigration and Customs Enforcement, Jesse had nearly blown his last assignment and thought he'd never get the chance to restore his reputation and career.

But ICE's bulk cash and smuggling division decided Helms Ice and Trucking Company was hot—laundering money for the Mexican cartel—and they wanted someone on the inside. Since the trucking company also had a catering side business specializing in ice sculptures, Jesse was it.

He shoved his hand through his hair. God had some sense of humor.

Miguel grinned as he assisted Jesse in closing off the back of the truck. He signaled to the driver that the truck was ready to go, and it lumbered away from the loading dock.

"You okay today?" Miguel asked.

"Everything's great," Jesse lied. With his superiors breathing down his neck, he had to come up with something and soon. He'd already been working undercover too long for his own good.

"You'd better get back to your hole. You got another gig in a few days." Miguel strode over to a counter and grabbed a pack of cigarettes.

Though Miguel referred to the ice-sculpture competition that Jesse needed to prepare for, Jesse was concerned about a far different gig, and that's what had him on edge today. He was desperate to get in on what he believed would be the next transport of bulk cash. As the truck departed, Jesse fought the tensing in his gut. Could this truck be driving off with millions in cash tucked away behind or in the ice, and Jesse had somehow missed it?

Carlos returned from his break. "We expecting another truck in a few?"

"You're not going anywhere. Jesse's got his own work. You're lucky he was here to cover for you," Miguel said.

Carlos gave a halfhearted snarl. Jesse didn't like the guy. After years spent working undercover assignments, Jesse had learned there were some people you met while undercover that you grew to care about and others you grew to hate. Carlos was someone to hate. He had no doubt that Carlos was capable of much worse than smuggling cash. He might have committed the murder on the loading dock that occurred several months ago, bringing the police down on this place and the cash smuggling operations to a complete halt for a few weeks.

Jesse had to remain and bide his time until things began moving again. Though he had proof of several small transactions, those crimes had already occurred. His goal was to gather intelligence, figure out all the players and be witness to the movement of a large amount of cash—catching them in the act. This would bring stiffer penalties under federal law.

When Carlos's eyes slid toward him, Jesse turned his back on the man. "Later," he said, and headed for the exit.

He squeezed his eyes closed for a moment. Guys like Carlos were the reason Jesse had grown to loathe working undercover. Memories from his last assignment flooded his mind—a man struggling with the thugs of a drug ring Jesse had infiltrated. He'd lived with the nightmare day and night. Jesse could have stepped into the fray, but that would have been kicking his cover in the teeth. He'd almost cracked under the moral dilemma. If only Jesse had gone a little out of his way, he could have prevented the man from strolling around the corner at that precise moment—the exact wrong moment. He would never allow that to happen again.

He promised himself then that once he got out, he'd never go back. In the end, he'd almost blown the mission and been reprimanded before being returned to a desk job. After months living life undercover as a drug runner, learning to walk and talk like them, to avoid the cops, he'd struggled to fit in with his fellow agents again.

What had the psychiatrist told him? *"You're suffering from anxiety and extreme suspiciousness."* That he was near the breaking point.

A shiver swept over him when he passed the room-size freezer that took up a quarter of the loading dock. At the moment, he felt like he was near the freezing point—if he worked like this for much longer, his heart would turn stone-cold.

Right now, he knew one thing—if he wanted to transfer programs within the agency, he'd have to earn back the respect of his supervisors and the confidence of his fellow agents.

In order to do that he'd have to see this case through and make the bust of these so-called untouchables.

Nothing or no one would stand in his way this time. Nor would he allow anyone to stumble upon Carlos and Miguel on the loading dock. Not again. Not on his watch.

Casey Wilkes stood outside a door with a nameplate indicating it was the ice-sculpting studio, which she presumed was where she could find the ice sculptor. After knocking and receiving no response, she jiggled the doorknob.

Locked.

She forced her shoulders back, unwilling to give in to defeat. The receptionist probably lied to get rid of Casey, telling her the ice sculptor was here. The cute little brunette had been instructed not to allow visitors beyond the foyer, but Casey had pulled a trump card—she was the owner's niece, and needed an interview.

Casey didn't mention that until this week, she'd lived in a little town near Portland, Oregon—a far cry from Orange Crossings near San Diego—and had never been to the ice company before. Nor did she mention that John Helms had married her aunt three years ago, and Casey didn't know him that well.

She had no idea if Uncle John would allow her to get an interview, but since he and Aunt Leann were out of the country, traveling in Europe somewhere, and everyone else was leaving for the day or had already gone, there wasn't anyone around to question.

The receptionist didn't want to get fired for denying the owner's niece entry.

Casey looked down the hallway where she'd just walked. Helms Ice and Trucking Company conducted business from a large multifaceted warehouse, part of which had been converted into an office complex. Maybe the guy was around here somewhere.

Get the interview with the sculptor and you have a job.

The newspaper editor's words emboldened her, propelling her through a door and down another hallway where a few people remained working in their offices. A couple of women chatted and laughed when they passed her in the corridor— probably heading home for the day since they both held their purses—only giving her a cursory glance.

"Excuse me," Casey said.

The ladies paused and glanced back, as though uncertain Casey was talking to them.

"I'm looking for Jesse Dufour, the ice sculptor. He's not in his studio. Any ideas where I can find him?"

"Can't help you. Although..." The tall slender woman paused and stared at the ceiling for a moment as though gathering her thoughts. "His sculptures have to be delivered at some point, so try the loading dock."

"Thanks." Casey turned and walked in the opposite direction before it occurred to her she wasn't sure where to find the loading dock.

An unmarked exit and dark corridor later, she heard a voice behind a door and decided to ask for help. This was getting ridiculous.

After a quick, light knock, she opened the door to a small dimly lit room cluttered with papers strewn on empty desks and rank with the smell of cigarette smoke. A man stood in a shadowed corner, talking on his cell.

Finally. Relieved, she waited for him to notice her. As soon as he did, he stopped talking and skewered her with his gaze.

She shivered and sensed the sudden chill had nothing to do with the cold room.

Casey offered an apologetic look for interrupting his private communication and began backing from the room. Wait. He could answer a simple question.

"I'm sorry to bother you. Can you point me to the loading dock?"

The man scowled and pointed at the door. Casey frowned. Maybe she should have asked a different question.

As she made her way down a long corridor devoid of life and through another doorway, she prayed she would run into friendlier natives who could help her find the loading dock, or at least tell her where to find the ice sculptor.

In the shadows between boxes stacked to the ceiling, the only light streamed from a small window in a thick door of—if she had to guess, she'd say a giant freezer. She dropped her bag onto a box to give her shoulder a brief reprieve and examined the digital thermometer next to the door. Fifteen degrees. Definitely, it was some sort of cold storage room. She trembled.

This place was a veritable maze, and though as a seasoned reporter she hated to admit it, now she was lost.

From behind, a hand clamped her shoulder.

Her heart ricocheted. She jerked around to find a man with piercing blue eyes staring back. Though the look on his face was anything but friendly, relief swept through her.

For a fleeting moment, she feared Will Tannin had caught up with her. In almost the same manner, Tannin had grabbed her from behind and detailed how he planned to torture then kill her. Her throat constricted at the memory.

She'd fled Oregon that night a week ago.

But this man didn't have the look of a crazed killer. She should know. Her breathing slowed, if only a little.

"What are you doing here?" he asked.

Taken aback at his guarded tone, Casey struggled for words. "I'm sorry, I—"

"You shouldn't be here. Let's go." He glanced over her shoulder at something behind her, a sense of urgency in his eyes, and grabbed her arm. "The loading dock is off-limits to visitors. It isn't safe. You could get hurt."

Ah, so she'd at least found the loading dock. A small comfort.

Maintaining his hold on her, he tried to lead her away.

Casey stood her ground, attempting to tug her arm free. "Hey, you don't have to drag me."

"You'll follow me out?" He took his time slipping his hand away, looking into her eyes for assurance that she would obey.

"Of course. Why wouldn't I?" This was weird. Could Tannin have sent him? Dread stalked through her.

No. This insane fear of Tannin had to stop right now.

Again, he glanced behind her, deep lines of concern creasing his brow. She followed the guy into the corridor and then into an empty office. She figured he was escorting her somewhere "safe" to talk.

Once inside, she turned around to face him. He was closing the door. "Wait a minute. What are you doing?"

He ran a hand down his face. "The question is who are you and what were you doing trespassing?"

She opened her mouth to reply, but he had her there. "My name is Casey Wilkes. I'm a reporter

here to do a story on the ice sculptor. That's all."
She cringed inside. Since she was trying to fall off
the grid, she'd have to remember to use her recently
assumed pen name, Carson Williams.

While he appeared to contemplate her words, she
studied him. If they'd met on different terms, she
might have found him attractive. Scratch that. Regardless of the terms, he was good-looking. Thick
dark hair, troubled but intense blue eyes and a strong
clean-shaven jaw. She'd experienced firsthand that
he was strong and muscular. Heat crawled up her
neck.

Casey blew out a breath.

For a moment, she thought his expression might
have softened but it hardened again. "A reporter,
huh? That still gives you no right—"

"I'm sorry. I got lost and ended up on the loading
dock. Why don't you just ask me to leave?"

"All right. Would you please leave?"

Something about his actions weren't tracking,
but Casey didn't want to leave. Not really. She'd
come here for a reason. She stomped to the door
and placed her hand on the knob.

He put his hand over hers, sending a warm shudder through her. She yanked it back.

"Not so fast," he said.

"You can't keep me here." Her defiant words
mocked her. He *could,* actually, and that scared her.

This time his gaze softened. "Look, if you want

an interview with the ice sculptor, all you have to do is ask."

Casey felt like an idiot. He was right, and she wanted to explain, to start over. "The receptionist sent me back to look for him. But he wasn't in the studio, so…"

His mouth quirked in a grin and he crossed his arms, leaning against the door. She'd bet that was on purpose. "So, you thought you'd explore. What could it hurt, right? You might uncover the scoop of the century."

She hadn't gotten where she was today… Queasiness swirled inside. Where exactly was she today in her rising career as an investigative reporter?

Running for her life.

Still, his playful tone managed to bring a smile to the corner of her mouth. "Something like that." She wanted to kick herself. *Oh, I am not responding to his flirting! Nix this.*

He thrust his hand out. "I'm Jesse Dufour, the ice sculptor."

Casey stared for a full fifteen seconds, she was sure. "You're the sculptor?"

"That's right."

Her hands flew to her hair, and she ran her fingers through, making sure it was in place. She hated herself for primping in front of him.

He smiled, revealing not one, but two dimples in each cheek. She needed a diversion and started to reach for her bag. "My purse. I must have left it…"

He frowned a little too much for Casey's comfort. What was going on here?

"Promise me you'll stay here, and I'll give you that interview. I'm going to retrieve your bag."

She opened her mouth to ask him what was so dangerous about the loading dock. Why did she get the feeling he was sneaking around? Then she thought better of it, offering him a soft smile. "I promise."

That seemed to reassure him because he sent her a quick nod and left the room, closing the door behind him.

Mr. Jesse Dufour had just tangled with the wrong woman. The wrong reporter. Except, she couldn't go there. Not now. Not after everything that had happened after writing that exposé about Will. At least not until the trouble she'd stirred up had died down.

She'd come here today to meet the company's ice sculptor, arrange an interview, a simple story to fill newspaper space. Still, in her experience, simple stories weren't always that easy and this one had already grown complicated. She'd proven herself good enough at stirring up trouble. Maybe she could be equally as good at staying out of it. One simple story and she'd have this job.

An interview with the ice sculptor and coverage of the upcoming competition. That's all.

To that end, she'd have to ignore all the signals that there was something a little threatening going on here. Forget the look that could kill from the man on his cell. Forget that Jesse Dufour's strange demeanor and worried frown only intensified the sense of suspicion in her gut. This could mean a much deeper story. Adrenaline coursed through her. This could be her chance to get her life back—under a different name.

Or, she could lose her life completely. Hadn't she just driven over a thousand miles to escape a man who wanted her dead? Digging into his life for a story had been a mistake. But how could she have known?

Casey sighed and tugged the chair from the desk, plopping down.

It would be hard, but this time—if there was a story—Casey would let the truth lie buried. She had enough trouble already.

TWO

Jesse exited the room and stepped into the corridor, easing the door shut behind him. He prayed she would stay put but wasn't sure God would listen to the likes of him.

Hopefully, the woman hadn't just blown six months of work.

Because he'd had to stand idly by and watch people abused too many times at the hands of those he investigated, he reassured himself that he was justified in removing her, albeit a little brusquely. It could end up saving her life. But he'd created a new problem, because now he'd assured her an interview. What might she uncover about him? His real name, Jesse Mitchell?

He sighed and shoved open the door to the loading dock to retrieve her bag, hoping he'd find it before anyone else.

Carlos stood with Miguel, holding up a woman's shiny black bag—big enough that it could have been a briefcase—and scowling. Jesse meandered toward them, forcing a lazy grin as he formulated a cover story plus a back-up plan in case they didn't buy it.

Carlos dropped the bag to his side a little behind him and postured to block Jesse. "You know something about this?"

Jesse smiled and reached around Carlos for the bag, never taking his gaze from the man's eyes. "Sure, a woman got lost. I escorted her out. What? You've been looking for a bag just like this one? You want to keep it?"

Carlos and Miguel eyed each other then burst out laughing.

Miguel slapped Jesse on the back and squeezed his neck. Jesse couldn't afford to show his relief. He needed to keep his cool like he hadn't been concerned to begin with. Unlike how he'd handled the reporter.

"That's why I like you, Jesse. You make me laugh."

Over the past few months, Jesse and Miguel had become friends. Miguel called them brothers. Just another reason for Jesse's gut to sour every day. Growing close to people, becoming like family, then turning traitor on them was a tough gig.

Jesse held up the bag and laughed, too. "You want to look inside?" He feared they might already have done that, but then again, if she'd carried some sort of recording device or anything reporter-looking, they'd be having a different conversation right now.

"Nah. What do you think, I'm a criminal?" With that Miguel laughed again, mischief in his eyes.

"Hey, Elena wants you over for dinner again. You like her cooking, *sí?*"

Jesse scratched his chin as though he'd have to contemplate his answer. Miguel narrowed his eyes. Jesse allowed a broad smile. "You know I do."

"We'll set it up. Oh, and little Rosita has a crush on you, so be nice when you see her."

A truck backed up to the enclosure, drawing Miguel and Carlos's attention away.

Despite the cold filtering from the refrigeration storing the ice, a drop of sweat trickled down Jesse's temple. Not good. Jesse was grateful the men had been pulled away before they'd noticed that he was nervous.

He exited the loading dock and made his way back to the office, wanting to give Casey Wilkes a few choice words but knowing he couldn't. Little did she know what she could have walked in on—a person didn't just walk in on Carlos and Miguel these days.

Jesse marched toward the door, steadying his hands. He gripped the knob, hoping she'd waited like he asked, but if she wanted her bag she'd be there. Stepping inside, he smiled when he saw her sitting in the chair, her feet propped on the empty desk. He wondered what she'd say if he told her the man who used to occupy this office was dead, had been knocked off at this very company.

Upon seeing him, she grinned and shoved her gorgeous blond hair behind her shoulders.

"Well, you going to give me that?" Amusement filled her sea-green eyes.

"Uh, yeah. Sorry."

Here it comes. Now that she'd had a few minutes to catch her breath, she was going to ask him questions about the dangers of the loading dock. Fortunately, he had at least five things he could list that didn't include Carlos and Miguel.

She moved around the desk and stood next to him, offering her hand, bright pink polish on her nails. "It was nice to meet you, Mr. Dufour. I realize I must have caught you at a bad time today. We got off to a bad start. Sorry for that— " she cleared her throat, a mischievous smile playing on her lips "—inconvenience. In addition to an interview, I'd love to stop by and watch you create your sculptures as you prepare for the big ice-sculpture competition."

Jesse rubbed his jaw. Why wasn't she grilling him? She had to be up to something more. Her light floral perfume wrapped around him while he studied her. He took a step away to distance himself and crossed his arms, leaning against the wall and gaining some control over whatever magic she was working.

If she wasn't going to ask, he was going to offer. He couldn't have a reporter leave the premises without an explanation, even if it wasn't the complete truth. He didn't want to think about what she could do with that.

"Listen, about the loading dock."

She held up her hand, stopping him. "No need to explain again. Really. The loading dock is dangerous. You might want to post a warning sign to that effect. Then again, I got lost. Maybe a map of the entire facility would work better."

Incredulous, he almost choked on a laugh. Was she for real? He held up his hands in surrender. "Look, I'm sorry you got lost and that I had to escort you out."

He hoped she would leave it at that, satisfied that the loading dock was dangerous.

He liked her spirit, and he wanted to believe her story. That she'd gotten lost. That would keep things simple because what he didn't need right now was a reporter snooping around.

The last person to cross Carlos and Miguel had been silenced—he had either stumbled upon them in the middle of a delivery and was at the wrong place at the wrong time, or he'd been part of the crime ring and had given them reason enough to get rid of him. The empty office where he stood with Casey attested to the fact.

Her eyes narrowed if only a little before she flashed a smile, but he didn't miss it. "You're giving me an interview, Mr. Dufour, so we'll call it even."

Now it was Jesse's turn to narrow his eyes. Did she suspect something?

Casey held her smile in place while Jesse opened the door for her. "When can I come back for the interview, then?"

"I'll be starting on a sculpture for the competition in a couple of days. Come back then and we'll talk. Just stay outside of the loading dock." He smiled down at her as she strolled through the doorway, passing him, and she caught a whiff of his cologne. Nice.

"I'll escort you out this time so you won't get lost," he said, closing the door behind him. "Next time, I'll show you the side entrance to my studio."

He kept pace with her as they made their way down the long corridor. Several doors along this hallway had windows, and Casey glanced through each one as they passed.

"What exactly does Helms Ice and Trucking do? Well, besides create ice sculptures," she asked.

Jesse chuckled. "The ice division of the company makes and delivers ice, including dry ice, all over Southern California. The trucking side delivers frozen goods via refrigerated semis."

"And which division do ice sculptures fall under?"

"I'm on the ice side, or rather, a small catering side. The competition I've been asked to enter is part of the company's efforts to grow that part of the business. It's good publicity."

"Is there more than one ice sculptor, then? Surely, you can't do all this alone."

"I have an assistant. Someone who works with me. I suppose if the demand for ice sculptures grows, we'd have to hire more, yes."

Casey found herself relaxing a little. He was easy to talk to. This was starting to feel more like the interview she'd wanted. He opened another door for her, and Casey walked into the reception area.

He followed her then leaned against the tall reception counter. The brunette receptionist who'd been there earlier was now gone.

"Well, I guess this is it, then," Casey said, feeling a little awkward, though she wasn't sure why. Too bad she couldn't interview him right now. Would the promise of an interview be good enough for her editor, Danny?

"For now." Jesse smiled, but the walls he'd momentarily dropped were up again. "Here's my card. Call me in a couple of days and I'll meet you here."

She wanted to watch him walk away, but it appeared he was intent on seeing her leave the premises. Again, she got the sense he wanted her gone—and fast.

Casey gave a little wave then exited the door.

Once in the parking lot, she hurried to her car and clambered in. She tossed her bag on the passenger seat and all the stuff inside—paper, gum wrappers and even her wallet—spilled onto the floorboard.

Casey couldn't reach her new TracFone, which

had slid to the floor on the other side of the seat, just out of reach.

Of course.

She got out of the car and walked around to the other side, opened the door and shuffled through the junk to get her cell.

After she scraped everything except her phone back into her bag, she shoved the length of her hair behind her shoulder and climbed back into the driver's side.

She skimmed the contacts listed.

But why? Force of habit, she supposed. Since fleeing Oregon, everything about her life had changed. She'd better get used to it.

Who was she going to call? Not Eddie Morris, her editor in Oregon who'd sent her away on a leave of absence until Will Tannin gave up on destroying her, taking the newspaper with him. What would she tell him? She had stumbled upon a possible exposé but she wasn't about to tackle it?

Maybe she should call Danny Garcia, the editor who'd promised to hire her if she could get this story about the ice sculptor. No. She'd savor her almost-job contingent on her almost-interview for a while.

Meg. Her best friend expected a weekly update. But Meg could wait.

Casey needed to catch her breath. Gather her thoughts. She rested her head against the seat to take a calming breath. Could it actually have been a week ago that she'd driven all the way from Oregon to a little town on the outskirts of San Diego in order to hide?

Or "fall off the grid," as Eddie had put it.

Once settled in Aunt Leann's home, she'd marched right into the office of the *Orange Crossings Times* to ask for a job. As it turned out, the editor was in the midst of chewing out one of his reporters because he'd not been able to breach the gatekeeper at Helms Ice and Trucking Company. With the ice-sculpture competition approaching next week, he needed a story.

All Casey had to do was tell him she could get the story because her uncle owned the company. Since it was a simple human-interest story there wouldn't be any conflict of interest.

His response? If she got the story, she had a job.

She opened her eyes and noticed someone watching her from the far corner of the building. Black hair flashed then disappeared. She recognized him. The cell-phone guy. The worker had been watching her.

Her pulse inched up.

Why would he be watching her?

Or had Casey's stalker experience with Tannin put her reporter instincts on overdrive, and she was simply having knee-jerk reactions to everyone who so much as glanced her way?

Would she ever recover?

Shifting her lime-green Volkswagen bug into

Reverse, she backed out of the parking space and exited the lot as fast as her car would go.

Although disappointed she couldn't get an interview with Jesse today, she knew these things took time, and she'd see him again in a couple days. She allowed a smile to come to her lips when she remembered his rugged face and fierce blue eyes, teasing her. He'd actually had the audacity to flirt with her.

He had charm, that was a fact. The guy was dangerous in more ways than one. She turned on the radio, shoving thoughts of Jesse the ice sculptor aside as she headed to her aunt's beach house, just up the road from the ice company. She would call Meg when she got there.

Taking a left onto Shoreline Road, the frontage road that led to the beach, she continued to watch her rearview mirror, looking for a tail—a habit she'd gotten into while fleeing Oregon. She didn't think she'd ever lose it.

In three minutes she could relax behind the safety of the beach-house walls, alarm system on alert.

She pulled into the driveway and then all the way into the garage. While the automatic garage door began its slide to the ground, shutting her off from the neighbors, she glanced at her rearview mirror and noticed a man across the street, replacing a window in a house. He was watching.

Relax. He was probably curious if not suspicious. Completely normal.

Once inside, she kicked off her shoes. Though at first she planned to call Meg, the view of the ocean drew her forward. The wall on the west side of the house was nothing but a huge window, affording an amazing panoramic look at the beach, waves lapping the shore.

Any other time, she'd walk out onto the deck and let the salt-water breeze lick her skin. But not today.

A year ago, Casey had been conducting research on an article in which she hoped to expose the enormous salaries of heads of charities and non-profit organizations. Little did she know that in the process she'd be led down a money trail, following the money behind one Will Tannin, CEO of Inner City Aid in Portland, Oregon, and discover his duplicity. Tannin had an affair with a woman who'd sought aid through the organization. She'd given birth to his son, and though he refused to acknowledge the relationship, he paid the woman to keep quiet.

Casey hadn't gathered the evidence she needed to prove the money he paid the woman had come from the charitable funding, but she'd been working on that when she'd had to leave Oregon. Since Casey's exposé, Tannin had lost his job, his wife and family and his home. Though he had not been charged with a crime yet, his life had been destroyed.

Four months ago, Tannin began his attempt to systematically destroy Casey's life and had progressed to disrupting her career and credibility. His first act began when she discovered the hard drive on her home computer destroyed along with all backup files. Then her email had been hacked, and no matter how many times she changed the service provider or her password, her email address was used as spam to send pornography. So, she could live without email for a while.

The little things began to add up. Though the police could not identify the perpetrator, Casey knew it was Tannin. He'd threatened to destroy her life little by little.

She no longer answered her phone. No matter what the caller ID said, even if it was a friend calling, she would hear only the heavy breathing until she hung up. Tannin had called in a serious favor or paid someone in the world of hackers who knew what they were doing.

But why? Why would anyone go to that much trouble? Maybe Tannin had wondered the same about her unraveling his life.

Fine. She'd keep digging until he was arrested. But during the digging she discovered something else about Tannin—for years he'd been under the care of a psychiatrist for antisocial personality disorder, or rather, he was an abusive psychopath.

She'd done an exposé on the wrong man   Will Tannin had snapped. She would have done less harm by taking a baseball bat to a nest of killer bees.

The small interruptions in her everyday life were a nuisance, but a week ago, Tannin had hacked into the newspaper, changing a story she'd written in order to damage her professionally. Eddie had then told her to get out until everything died down. The newspaper couldn't afford to fight off a madman, especially when the police could find no proof to arrest him.

That's when Tannin had gone the next step and explained to Casey how and when he would kill her.

THREE

To be safe. That's all she really wanted.

She'd made the right decision to come here. Her mother and father had been killed in a car accident years ago, and Aunt Leann was the only real family Casey had left. Her aunt had had the foresight to send Casey the key to their home on the beach while she and Uncle John traveled Europe. Casey had taken the key and grabbed a few necessary items then fled her home, her friends and her job.

Casey tugged out one of the low-caloric frozen dinners she'd stocked the fridge with yesterday and shoved it into the microwave, thinking she needed to find out more about the ice company.

She sighed, knowing she had to quit her insane need to uncover a story, no matter the cost. While she ate her dinner, she began the process of creating a completely new email screen name. One more step away from Tannin.

Relaxing against the chair back, she rolled her

shoulders, easing the tension in her neck. The view from the living-room window had grown dark. She hadn't noticed that night had fallen.

Casey rose calmly from the dinner table where she'd set up a temporary office with her laptop, and moved to the large window that provided the ocean view. She stared out, again, only this time instead of seeing waves lapping the shore, complete darkness stared back along with her reflection. The sun had set, and she'd missed the moment.

She turned the lights down in the house, hoping to gain a better look outside without her reflection. For a few seconds, she searched the blackness, but could see nothing except a few lights in the distance—probably a fishing boat or two. She wondered if Tannin could be out there somewhere, watching her. She couldn't shake off the sense that someone was, in fact, observing her.

Despite everything she'd been through, the idea still seemed a little paranoid. After all, she'd driven almost twenty hours, putting over a thousand miles distance between her and Tannin. He couldn't know where in the country she was.

The strangeness of today fresh on her mind, she shoved the hair from her face, wondering if she might have something more than Will Tannin to worry about.

"Get the interview and you've got a job," Danny had said.

Get in and get out, leave the rest of it buried.

She began the chore of tugging the heavy window treatments over the vast expanse of glass until it was completely covered.

A sound from somewhere in the house startled her. Casey froze.

Holding her breath, she listened and heard the noise again. She spotted a large ballerina figurine on the end table. She could use it as a weapon if needed. She lifted it.

It was heavy enough.

It would do. Except… Was it a Lladro?

Casey cringed for half a second and looked around her for something less expensive, but there wasn't anything except pricey-looking décor and figurines accenting the room. She hadn't even noticed until now.

Aunt Leann would understand, since Casey's life could be at stake.

Jesse allowed the waves to wash up against his feet and ankles, soaking his running shoes, as he held the golden retriever's leash. He stared through his night-vision binoculars at John Helms's house, not seeing much now that Casey had closed all the curtains. Finally, he jammed them into the pack he wore around his waist and continued his jog, Simon at his side.

She'd looked out into the darkness, a strange expression on her face, before tugging the curtains to the center of the window from one side and then moving to the far side to start the process over again. He'd watched her the entire time. Her trim figure didn't seem equal to the task, but she managed. There was something in the way she acted when she closed the curtains, like she expected someone was watching her—and little did she know that he was.

Beautiful blond strands hung around her face, her expression one of both defiance and fear—not much change from when he'd come across her on the loading dock and rescued her. Though she probably didn't think of it like that.

Why was John Helms's niece staying in his home while he was gone? Not so unusual—but then why had she appeared to slink onto the loading dock in need of an interview with him? At the time he had been inclined to believe her explanation, wanted to believe it, if he were honest. Anything more would be trouble. Then he'd found out about her background.

An investigative reporter.

She was trouble or she was going to get into trouble. Jesse hadn't figured out which, but he now had the added assignment to thwart in either case.

Beautiful...but dangerous. Those same words had come to mind when he thought about dry ice. The comparison elicited a small grin.

He drew in rhythmic breaths as he jogged up the beach away from the house, considering what tomorrow would bring. Jesse was close to being someone Miguel would finally trust and accept into the inner circle of those operating the cash-smuggling ring.

With Casey Wilkes's appearance on the scene, Jesse was now in the position of also having to infiltrate her life without her knowing his motives—but to protect her, to protect the covert assignment.

Another person he'd have to lie to. Another person whose trust he would need to win, and who would end up hating him in the end.

Lungs burning, Jesse dropped to his knees, catching his breath. He wanted this to be over and done with. He wanted out. But now things were more complicated.

Simon whined and licked Jesse's face. Jesse pulled away, wanting to cry out to God. He needed God's help, but it had been so long since he felt good enough to be on speaking terms with the Almighty.

Jesse squeezed sand in his fists, his instincts on fire. He wasn't about to let this attractive woman reporter ruin this assignment.

A scream ripped through the night.

Casey fought against the arms that wrapped around her, screaming and kicking.

In the hallway outside the guest bedroom she slammed the figurine at the man's head, but missed.

He squeezed her wrist, sending pain up her arm. She cried out and the figurine flew through the air then slid across the floor of the bedroom.

Her only weapon gone.

The wall! She tried to reach the wall with her feet. Shove her back into the man and loosen his grip.

If she could just gain traction. There.

Her feet against the wall, she pressed hard, slamming him into the corner of the hallway. He cursed.

She pressed harder, but his grip around her only tightened. She couldn't breathe. He shifted and dragged her down the hall.

His grip loosened but only slightly. She drew in a breath. "What are you doing? Where are you taking me? Let me go."

Now she wished she'd made friends with the neighbor.

Casey screamed again, louder this time, if possible.

Then, to her surprise, he threw her on the floor. She slammed against the tile, hitting her head.

The taste of blood filled her mouth. Unsure why he'd dropped her, but not caring, Casey scrambled to her feet. Before she took off running, she glanced behind her.

The man wore a tailored black suit, she now noticed. He reached into his suit jacket and pulled something out.

Casey gasped.

A gun. He had a gun.

Casey's knees trembled. "What are you going to do?"

* * *

Like a bull intent on goring his target, Jesse slammed into the man from the side. Though he'd held Casey at gunpoint, the guy hadn't fingered the trigger guard yet. Jesse had to act fast.

The nine-millimeter slid across the floor.

The man grunted from the blow. Jesse landed on top of him as they hit the tile floor. The attacker moaned, but Jesse didn't care. He threw a punch in his face for good measure.

Blood gushed from the man's nose, and he pressed his hands to it. "You broke my nose," he said, his nasal-sounding tone filled with outrage.

Jesse held his fist in the air and paused. "I'm going to break more than that. Who are you and what are you doing here?"

Still cupping a hand over his nose, the man dropped to his knees. Something slid from his pocket.

"The name is Harrison Spear. I'm a friend of the Helmses and I came to check on the house. I found her inside, stealing from them. I pointed the gun at her so she would stay there while I called the police. The bigger question is who are you? And who is she?"

Fire in her eyes, Casey stepped forward. "I was doing no such thing." She fairly spat at the man.

"Come on, you had that figurine. It's worth a lot of money."

Jesse relaxed, but only slightly. "Look, I think there's been a misunderstanding."

He looked to Casey, knowing he'd eventually need to explain why he'd been here to save the day.

"My name is Casey Wilkes and I'm Leann Helms's niece." Casey's face went pale as she gripped the table. "What were you doing sneaking around in the house? I didn't hear you come in."

Jesse rushed to her side and grabbed her arms, supporting her. Holding tightly, he guided her to the sofa.

To the stranger he said, "You can get out of here. I think you've done enough damage tonight, don't you?"

Jesse pulled out his phone, acting as if he was making a call, but took a picture of the man before he left the house. He made a mental note that Spear had grabbed the gun on his way out, but left the item that had fallen from his pocket. He must not have realized he'd lost it. Jesse would remember it, though.

"Thank you." The soft words drew Jesse's attention back to the woman at his side.

He squeezed her hand, hoping to reassure her, and felt the strength in her grip. "You're welcome. I'm just glad—" What exactly could he say to her?

"Glad that you were here? You want to explain that?" Her tone held only a hint of accusation.

Jesse stood, wanting to put distance between himself and the beautiful Casey Wilkes. He held up a finger. "Just a second."

He went to the back door and unlocked then opened it, whistling. Initially, he'd come through the front door, which was unlocked, presumably by Spear, unless Casey had left it unlocked. A glance back and he witnessed Casey's raised eyebrows.

Simon came bounding into the house.

Jesse laughed and rubbed his dog behind the ears. "Simon and I jog on this beach every evening. I heard a scream."

Simon sprang over the sofa and onto Casey. He licked her, causing laughter to erupt. The sound of it warmed Jesse. As he watched her petting Simon, he knew that she'd recovered from having a gun pointed at her. She'd be all right—at least this time.

Soon enough he'd find out if Spear was criminally involved in the smuggling ring, working with Miguel or Carlos, or if he really was checking on the house for the Helms. Still, how had he gotten in unnoticed? Was he already here when Casey arrived home? For his own cover, he'd given Spear no reason to suspect he was anything other than Casey's friend—he'd done exactly what a friend would do.

Casey looked up at Jesse, breaking into his disturbing thoughts. Unable to look away, he held her gaze a little too long. In that instant, he felt a strong connection to her.

Not good.

FOUR

The trauma of the last few minutes still fresh in her mind, Casey ran her fingers through Simon's soft fur and looked into Jesse's face.

Pain seeped into her thoughts. She remembered hitting the tile with her head and biting the inside of her mouth. She frowned and touched her head.

"You're hurt." Jesse nudged the dog from the sofa and sat next to her. "Let me see."

He placed his hands on her head, tilting it just so, then ran a finger over the lump. "Ouch..." he said, as though her pain were his.

Though she winced a little, his gentle touch and apparent concern sent a barrage of warmth through Casey's insides. Uncomfortable with his nearness, she pulled away. "It's nothing. Just a bump."

He shoved his hand over his mouth, a contemplative look on his face. "Maybe we should take you to the E.R., just to be safe."

Casey pushed up from the sofa. "I'm fine. I've had a concussion before, and this is nothing."

When Simon began sniffing around the living room, Jesse rose and moved toward the dog. He reached down and grabbed the leash then looked over at Casey. "What can I do to help? Can I get you something?"

She weaved her fingers through her hair, careful to avoid the sore spot. "I'm just a little shaken, that's all. It's not every night a girl faces off with a man holding a gun in her own home." She offered a small grin. "Even if it isn't exactly my home."

"Maybe you should call your aunt and uncle and let them know what happened."

"Yeah, let them call off any other dogs." Feeling chilled, Casey rubbed her arms and turned her back on Jesse. Tonight's incident, coupled with fleeing her home only days ago, left her more than frazzled. Tears stabbed at the back of her eyes.

From beside her, a strong arm wrapped around her shoulders and squeezed. "It's all right, Casey." Jesse's words were soft, his breath warm against her ear.

This wasn't the man she met today on the loading dock. This was someone entirely different. She liked this Jesse much better.

Casey wanted to ask him how he knew it was all right, but she couldn't because he would hear the tears in her voice as she fought them sliding down her cheeks. At least she didn't fall victim to a full sob, which is what she really wanted to do.

She couldn't be that uninhibited in front of

Jesse—a man she'd met only this afternoon. By all counts, he was a complete stranger.

And yet, Casey felt safe with him. Because of that, she allowed him to hold her, if only for a few moments. She sank into what felt like the protective armor of his arms. It had been far too long since she'd experienced that feeling.

Finally, her anguish dissipated, at least for now, she released a slow breath. Jesse must have taken that as his cue and dropped his arms.

He turned her to face him and lifted her chin. "You're going to be all right. Make sure you set the alarm when I leave."

Casey wanted to tell him that arming the place hadn't stopped the intruder. But then again, Mr. Spear wasn't exactly an intruder and obviously had the alarm-system password. She'd have to ask Aunt Leann if she could change the password and how to do it. That would go a long way in making her feel safer.

"Thank you, Mr. Jesse Dufour. Who knows what might have happened if you hadn't shown up." She knew her smile was weak, but Jesse was the only reason she smiled at all. That is, Jesse and his dog, Simon.

He jammed a hand in his pocket and held Simon's leash, keeping the dog from her, then without warning, he released him. Simon came bounding at Casey once again.

She knelt to meet him. "Come here, you."

When she looked up at Jesse, his expression had sobered. "I'm going to check around the rest of the house now to make sure there isn't someone else lurking in a closet, though I doubt it."

"I'll come with you," she said.

"No, you stay with Simon. He'll keep you safe if there's any need."

Jesse finally returned. "The house is empty except for us. Listen, I gave you my business card today, but it doesn't include my personal cell. Let me give you that number."

"I'll get my phone." Casey came back to find him standing halfway out the doorway, one foot on the deck. "Okay, what is it?"

He gave her the number and she stored it in her phone. "Got it. But I'm sure I'll be fine. It was just a misunderstanding, right?"

"Right. If you get another intruder you should call the police. I was referring to the fact that you wanted an interview. That's the best way to contact me." He grinned.

"I knew that." Heat crept up her neck. Had she actually thought he would return to protect her if she called? Still, he'd already given a contact number for the interview. Why was he giving his personal number now? She liked that. Warmth spread through her but it quickly died. She couldn't have called the police tonight if she tried. Or Jesse, either, for that matter.

Next time she'd go for the phone instead of a figurine.

"How about tomorrow at nine?" he asked.

"Tomorrow? I thought you said a couple of days?" Casey had considered that Jesse would likely renege, considering how eager he had been to see her leave the ice company.

"Okay, a couple of days then," he said.

Did she really want to wait that long? Not a chance.

"Tomorrow at nine o'clock."

"See you then." He completed his exit through the door.

She watched him make his way down the steps and disappear into the darkness on the beach. Suddenly she felt drained—tired from running for her life, running from Will, and exhausted from her struggle with a friendly intruder.

What an oxymoron.

Long after Jesse left that night, Casey lay in bed, staring at a late-night talk show on the muted television while she held the phone to her ear. She'd left a message with Aunt Leann about the friendly but brusque intruder, then spent a few minutes writing in her diary. She'd kept a diary for years. All of her deepest feelings were poured onto its pages, including thoughts about everyone she knew. When she'd fled Portland, her diary had been among the most important items to grab. Journaling kept her centered, giving her the ability to laugh when life threw her the unexpected. Maybe one day she could read back over the events of the last few months and laugh.

No. She doubted she'd ever laugh about this.

Then, she'd jammed the book beneath a pillow and called Meg because she couldn't bear to be alone tonight.

"Thanks for staying on the line with me, Meg. I think I'm finally getting sleepy."

"I'm glad you called. I was getting worried. But...I want to hear more about this Jesse guy. He really just barged into the place and tackled a guy with a gun? Who would do that?"

A hero, that's who.

Meg wanted Casey to focus on something positive so she could get some sleep, Casey knew that. She pointed the controller at the television and shut it off then snuggled deeper into the soft, quilted blankets.

Funny, earlier in the day she'd wanted to call Meg to tell her about the strange vibes she'd gotten from Jesse while at her uncle's company—how suspicious she'd been of him. She'd wanted to hear if Meg thought Casey was overreacting, given all she'd been through.

Now she considered Jesse one of the good guys, and she didn't need Meg's opinion to believe it.

But did that really matter when Will Tannin was

out there, waiting and watching for his chance to kill her? Despite the distance she'd put between her and Tannin, she couldn't shake the feeling that she hadn't lost him.

It was well after eleven-thirty when Jesse felt comfortable releasing his watch over the house where Casey was hopefully sleeping. After checking the house—looking for any places that an intruder could easily enter or had already entered—Jesse had said good-night and instructed her to arm the security system.

Though Spear claimed he wasn't an intruder, the incident had shaken Casey and, Jesse hated to admit, it had shaken him. He'd given a show of jogging down the beach but returned moments later to watch for signs of danger.

In the meantime, he sent the image he'd taken of Spear to the others working the case to be analyzed. He'd know soon enough if tonight's mishap had been just that...a case of mistaken identity. And a case in which Spear had been abusive in his handling of Helms's niece. Jesse sensed in his gut there was more going on here.

He tugged the thumb drive from his pocket—the item he'd seen slip from Spear's pocket. He intended to find out what was on it. Spear would soon discover he'd lost the item and if he had any sense, he'd suspect that it occurred during his scuffle with Jesse.

Jesse feared Spear would return to the house to

search for the missing item. What Jesse didn't know was the man's mood if he came back—would he knock on the door, knowing Casey was there, or would his handling of her be gruff again?

Right off, he didn't think he would like the guy even if he hadn't been pointing a nine-millimeter at Casey.

Casey opened her eyes and stretched out on the soft mattress—one of the best she'd ever slept on.

Oh, no. What time was it?

Blurry-eyed, she sat straight up and stared at the clock on the bedside table. Did that read nine o'clock?

Tossing the blankets off, Casey hurried to the bathroom to shower and dress. She had her interview with Jesse this morning and now she was late. She'd never overslept like this. But the last few days had been harrowing, and she hadn't given herself much time to regroup.

It was too late for a few days of rest now. She had a job, or was close to having one.

Dressed and as ready to face the day as she would be, Casey backed her car from the driveway, planning to grab a cup of coffee on the way to the Helms Ice and Trucking Company where she'd interview Jesse. Her heart did a quick flip at the idea of seeing him again.

Pathetic.

Her car struggled to climb the hill as she whipped

around a curve in the road that skirted a sea-cliff viewpoint. Steering with her left hand, she called the *Orange Crossings Times* on her phone with her right and, careful to watch the road, too, she punched in the editor's extension.

To her surprise, Danny Garcia picked up on the first ring.

"Danny here."

"Mr. Garcia, hi, this is Casey Wilkes, aka Carson Williams. I got that story you wanted."

"Oh, yeah? Which one was that?"

Casey held on to her smile, despite his discouraging tone.

"I'm headed over to interview Jesse Dufour, the ice sculptor at Helms Ice. So, do I have the job, then?"

Casey's car lurched out of control and she dropped her cell to grip the wheel.

What in the world?

The VW was nearly impossible to control. A car honked as it passed her on Shoreline Road.

Casey slowed the car, though steering was difficult, and managed to prod it onto the shoulder, though not completely.

She hopped out to investigate the damage. About a quarter of the car was still on the road. Too bad. With the crags hedging the beach next to the road and her inability to perfectly control the car, she didn't feel comfortable trying to move it completely off the road.

But on this side, she saw nothing wrong.

She stomped around to the other side.

A blowout.

Of all the...

Hands on her hips, she turned her gaze from the tire and her precarious position on the road and scanned the shoreline, watching the waves as they lapped the beach. The day had started wrong, all wrong.

Opening the passenger door, Casey scrounged around the small car looking for her cell that she'd dropped mid-conversation with Danny.

She found it and held it to her ear. "You still there?"

Silence. Casey called him again, but the line was busy. Next, she called Jesse's number, thankful he'd thought to give it to her, and that she'd stored it in her phone.

That he'd been that protective and concerned for her seemed a little strange at first. But with the likes of Tannin after her, Casey could use a dose of protective behavior from a man, so she had welcomed it. Last night, he'd single-handedly doused her suspicious first impression of him.

She was happy to nix any further thoughts on the matter, considering she had enough trouble already.

"Casey, where are you?" Jesse said, skipping right over the normal greeting.

Casey heard a note of alarm in his voice and wanted to dispel his concern. "I've got a flat tire.

Hope that doesn't inconvenience you. Can you wait for me?"

She left out that she was already running late when she woke up this morning.

"I'll do better than that. Tell me where you are, and I'll come change your tire."

Was he serious? Though in all honesty, she'd hoped for a little help. "Just up the..."

Casey paused mid-sentence and watched as a silver SUV took the curve in the road much too fast. What's more, even with her car in full view, it began picking up speed.

Really? Could they not see that her flower-girl green VW was parked partially on the road?

"Shoreline, not too..."

"What's the matter?" he asked. "Casey?"

"There's a car driving a little too fast." To avoid hitting her car they'd have to veer, and it looked like it was going to be one of those last-minute swerves, if it happened at all.

A prickle of alarm snaked up her spine.

To Casey's shock, the driver gunned the engine and veered right toward her car—and her.

FIVE

Casey's ear-splitting scream sliced through Jesse's mind.

He'd already jumped in his Jeep to drive over and change her tire, and now he peeled from the parking lot, through a red light, ignoring the honks and a near-collision with a minivan, and onto Shoreline Road.

"Casey, can you hear me? Are you there?" The connection was lost. He slung the phone into the seat next to him.

"God, if you can hear me, please, protect her." *Please, let her be okay.*

Guilt wrangled through him—why did it take a crisis situation for him to cry out to God, to actually ask for help?

He already knew the answer to that—he still wasn't sure God was listening. Jesse carried a lot of baggage, all due to his career. That's why it was more than critical for him to get it right this time.

A red Toyota Camry—someone out for a joy

ride—drove like a rickshaw in front of him. Jesse laid on his horn as if he believed they would pull over for him—which they didn't—then passed when he had the chance.

Not far up the road he spotted the green thing she called her car. From this distance, it appeared unharmed, but he couldn't be sure. And where was she? Had someone taken her?

His pulse ringing in his ears, he feared from the beginning that her simple stumble onto the loading dock, coupled with her background, might put her in a potentially explosive situation. If someone considered her a threat, the stakes were too high to allow Casey to simply walk away.

He intended to find out if Carlos and Miguel had plans to hurt her or worse, kill her.

But how could he find out? And if that were the case, how could he stop it?

Nearing her car, he slammed on the brakes, sending the Jeep sliding across the graveled shoulder. Jesse jumped out. Casey was nowhere to be seen.

He jogged from the VW to stand at the edge of the rocky face that tapered into a grass-covered knoll before morphing into sand. Cupping his hands, he shouted. "Casey!"

"You don't have to yell."

Jesse looked down. There she sat, at the bottom of a short drop, next to a moss-covered boulder.

"Casey!"

Relief washed over him like a twenty-foot wave.

He almost couldn't believe his eyes. He leaped down and closed the distance between them. Upon his approach, Casey stood, brushing off her slacks.

He'd honestly thought the worst. Overwhelmed to see her alive, he pulled her into his arms. She melted into him as he brushed his hand down her long, silky hair.

"I'm so glad you're all right," he said, a mere whisper against her ear. "What are you doing down here?"

Was she hiding? No, if someone wanted her they could easily have found her.

"After what happened, I needed to sit down. I found this spot."

Sensing it was time to let her go, he held her at arm's length. "You want to tell me why I heard you scream again? Because this is becoming a habit."

"Sorry. I certainly wouldn't want your coming to my rescue to be a habit." Her sea-green eyes pierced his.

Regretting his words, he asked again. "Casey, what happened?"

Her eyes shone with tears as she looked away.

He thought she was crying, except the hint of a smile touched her lips when her gaze returned to him. She'd had a scare, but she was rallying, at least he hoped.

He liked that.

But he had more important things to think about. Jesse hated considering that Casey had possibly become a target. She hadn't exactly done anything to deserve drawing the crime ring's attention. At least, not yet.

And if she had, then why was she still alive? Things weren't adding up.

"Tell me exactly what happened." He needed facts.

A warm breeze wafted over him, carrying her perfume with it.

"You already know half of it," she said. "I had a blowout then stopped to change it and that's when I called you. I was on the phone with you when I saw an SUV barreling toward the car and me."

"Are you sure it was barreling toward you, or simply gunning up the hill? It obviously didn't hit your car. Why would anyone want to hurt you? Could you be mistaken about the driver's intent?" Jesse cringed at his questions, knowing all the possibilities. But would she know? That's what he really needed to find out. Had she done something at the ice company that he knew nothing about?

Something to seriously stir things up?

"I don't know, Jesse. Another car came around the corner and the SUV corrected its course. You're probably right. It was nothing. I overreacted, and feel like an idiot now. But for a moment there, I really thought the driver intended…" She swallowed hard.

Noticing a slight tremble in her hands, Jesse hated to see her distressed yet again. Still, his shoulders relaxed, if only a little. Maybe it was a fluke, a result of Casey's nerves. He couldn't be certain that she was a target, at least not yet. He took a measure of relief from that.

"Did you get the license plate?"

Casey shook her head. "By the time they passed me, I had run out of the way. I don't think they even saw me. I'm not sure of the make or model, but I could probably figure it out if I looked at pictures."

If they hadn't seen her then it wasn't an attempt on her life. Did someone want to damage her car to send her a warning? Jesse wasn't sure her claims made any sense.

Jesse squeezed her arm and smiled—a meager attempt to help her recover. "The important thing is that you're all right. I'm going to change your tire now."

The limp smile she gave him in return told him she remained uncertain about what had happened. He would check for tampering when he examined the tire, and even if he found none, he'd make sure to get an expert opinion. Though Casey seemed on edge, she hadn't considered it a setup—a flat tire, then a hit-and-run.

His senses on alert, Jesse worked to change the tire while remaining acutely aware of his surroundings. For all he knew, if someone were trying to harm Casey, they would come back.

After replacing the blown tire with the spare, Jesse stood and wiped the sweat from his forehead.

The sun was beginning to climb high in the sky. Though temperatures in this region were usually a steady seventy degrees, no matter the season, Jesse felt the heat of his labor. He hadn't seen any obvious tampering, but that didn't mean anything.

"I'll get this replaced for you," he said, and carried the tire over to the back of his Jeep. He'd pass it to someone who could get it to Paul Scott in forensics.

Casey trotted behind him. "Really, that's not necessary. You've done so much already. I feel bad enough as it is for bothering you."

Jesse ignored her and shoved the tire in the back then shut the hatch. He leaned against the Jeep and crossed his arms. "Casey, relax. You're not bothering me. In fact, far from it."

He gave her an easy smile because he knew he needed to watch out for her, keep her near. He needed her to like him, even if it were based on a lie. For that, he hated himself.

Hated his job. But that didn't matter right now.

The problem was, he really did like her, was attracted to her, and that made things much more dangerous. An emotional connection could distract him.

"I hope you're still up for that interview," he said, and winked.

She frowned, sending a shard of disappointment through him. Maybe he was pouring it on too thick.

"Sure, but I haven't had my coffee yet this morning. I'm starting to feel the effects already."

"I've got just what the doctor ordered in my studio. Working with ice can chill a guy to the bone. I've got a fancy coffeemaker and all the fixin's."

Casey's smile coiled heat through his insides. He didn't think he'd need coffee with her around. A silence grew between them—both awkward and uncomfortable. He wanted to hold her again, but this time he had no clear reason other than wanting to feel her in his arms. The thought was ill-timed and inappropriate, and Jesse inwardly groused at himself.

The rumble of a vehicle drew his attention and through the Jeep windows, he spotted what looked like a navy blue SUV making its way up and around the incline.

Now he had a reason. He tugged her behind him as though he could hide her and if not, he could protect her with nothing more than his body. Yeah, right. "Casey, what color was the SUV you saw?"

At the first sign of trouble, he'd get her out of the way, but he didn't want to scare her anymore if it wasn't necessary.

"Silver."

Regardless of it not being the same vehicle, Jesse held her for a moment more, letting the vehicle pass. He almost wished it were the same one so he could get the license plate and find out what really happened, if there was a connection to the vehicle and the crime ring.

The fact that she'd had two close calls—though

they both appeared to be innocent misunderstandings—made his gut churn.

Casey followed Jesse in her car, grateful for his assistance. If only he could help her, really help her.

She hadn't told him the whole of it—she had a madman after her and that's why she was suspicious beyond reason. But why should she tell Jesse? Would he believe her? Or would he just think she was crazy because she'd been unable to prove anything? Nor had the police, bringing Casey to decide they had grown calloused to her accusations.

That's why, when Tannin explained how he would kill her—and she was surprised he had not done the deed right then and there—Casey didn't even consider calling the police. She'd simply fled town. Maybe that's all Tannin had wanted. As things stood, he'd lost everything and so had she.

The question still nagged her, though. Had Tannin found her in Orange Crossings? Had he been driving the SUV or was it, as Jesse suggested, a misunderstanding?

Translated, I'm paranoid.

Even if she wasn't overly suspicious, she could go crazy trying to figure things out.

Should she leave town? Where else could she go with no money and no place to stay?

Her sixth sense told her to stay right where she was. Jesse had done a pretty good job of keeping her safe since she'd arrived, and he didn't even have a clue she was in trouble.

Did that mean she was using the guy for protection? She allowed a chuckle. Not exactly something to be proud of.

She turned into the ice company's parking lot, following right behind Jesse, and parked next to him. Her emotions and heart were more than vulnerable right now. Desperate and on edge, she needed to tread carefully where one Jesse Dufour was concerned.

She'd known him for all of a day, but just being near him did funny things to her. Getting involved with him romantically would be nuts. He had no clue what he was getting into, and besides, at any moment she might have to run again. Nor did she know Jesse—he could be hiding dark secrets, as well.

Lost in her thoughts, Casey absently sat in her car and before she realized it, Jessie was opening the door for her. He offered his hand and she accepted, stepping from the car.

"Thanks." She tossed him a smile, but knew it was feeble.

"What's the matter? Changed your mind already?"

"No, just need the coffee. I'll be a hundred percent in no time," she said, unsure of her words.

She stood behind him as he jiggled his keys and found the right one to unlock a door.

"This is the side entrance to my studio," he said. "Much quicker access to the parking lot."

He shoved the door open and allowed her to enter before him.

She shuffled into the darkness, Jesse right behind her. He flipped the light switch and fluorescents began the familiar flickering hum and pop then lit the entire room—with a concrete floor, it looked more like part of the warehouse than an office. But then again, it was supposed to be a studio for sculpting ice.

Jesse swept his arm around. "This is where it's done."

"Really?"

"No." He laughed. "I usually sculpt the ice inside a refrigerated room where the temperature is a steady twenty degrees."

Casey shivered. "It feels cold enough in here for ice. I should have brought a jacket. What was I thinking?"

"That's my fault. I should have mentioned that to you. But, no problem. I've got that covered." He grabbed a jacket from a peg on the wall and handed it to her.

She slipped into what he offered, though it was three sizes too big. She'd roll up the sleeves if she weren't so cold. It would do.

"Have a seat, and I'll make a fresh pot of coffee." He motioned for her to sit in a plush-looking, contemporary-style chair. That was a surprise, considering the work benches and various tools and equipment scattering the room.

Was there a woman in Jesse's life already? Disappointment pressed down on her at the thought, although it wasn't her business.

She could ask that as part of the interview.

Casey did as he asked, recognizing that she was beginning to feel the strain of the past week—maybe she had survived this long on adrenaline alone—and she admitted she should have taken a few days to rest. But when she had first arrived in Orange Crossings, she'd wanted something to take her mind off almost becoming a murder victim, so she'd tackled the sculptor article.

Initially, she had believed herself to be safe here, and she desperately wanted to continue to believe that.

Connecting with Jesse appeared to have been beneficial, as well, and for now, she would play it safe and stick close to him. He hadn't said a word to her about calling the police on the near-miss today.

Probably thought she was crazy. And that was a real bummer. Casey frowned. She had to pull herself from these depressing thoughts.

Standing at the counter, he had his back to her as he fiddled with the coffeemaker. She took the opportunity to press her cheek against the collar of his jacket and she drew in a breath.

Jesse. His scent filled her head.

In the short time she'd known him, she had been

in his arms at least twice now. Distancing herself from the crazy whirlwind emotions, Casey reminded herself of the circumstances that had drawn her into his arms.

"How do you like it? Strong or weak?" His question broke into her morbid thoughts.

Casey realized he was staring at her. "Strong. I love a dark brew with a tablespoon of half-and-half."

He grinned. She could get used to that grin.

"A woman after my own heart."

Finally, Jesse made his way to Casey, holding a steaming mug of dark, rich coffee. "Maybe this will not only warm you but wake you up, too."

Casey widened her eyes and sat tall, taking the mug from his hands. "I'm not falling asleep."

Unease flickered across his eyes. "You didn't sleep last night after your uncle's friend accosted you in the house, did you?"

Unwilling to admit she hadn't slept all that well for an entirely different reason, Casey focused on sketches on the wall behind him. She was tired because of the traumatic days, weeks and months before yesterday—but she couldn't tell him about that, either. Still, she'd slept a little, she knew, because Jesse had made her feel a degree of safety. She smiled into her cup.

"It was a restless night," she finally said, and took a long swallow of Jessie's coffee. "You should go into the coffee business. I'd come to your coffee shop every day."

Jesse laughed. "That's what Ricky says."

"Ricky?"

"He's my assistant, helps me with the ice. I can't do everything without a few extra hands. But he's a floater, so sometimes he's here, sometimes he's helping out in another department."

"So, he's not an ice sculptor like you?"

"I'm not sure that's his aspiration."

"I've never seen one at work," she said. "An ice sculptor, that is."

"Then you're in for a real surprise. It isn't nearly as glamorous as one might think. If you're ready, follow me."

He led the way into another small office in the corner of the larger room where he'd made the coffee.

"Here's where I create conceptual drawings." Jesse showed her the artwork that he'd printed from a computer.

"There are some similar sketches on the wall out there," Casey said.

Jesse nodded. "Yes. I can tell how big I need to make the blocks of ice. I've been working a few days on preparing blocks for my next sculptures."

He gave her a quizzical look. "This is the sort of stuff you wanted to know, right? How it's all done?"

Casey nodded. "Well, that and I'll want to interview you personally. This is all very intriguing. Keep talking."

She tugged out a small notepad and her pen, wishing she had her camera.

Jesse tugged a navy blue hoodie over his head that said Helms Ice on the front and tossed a pair of gloves and a cap at Casey, then pulled a pair of thin white gloves over his hands.

"Follow me." He led her into another room connected to his office.

Casey stepped inside after him, realizing it was a refrigerated room. "Now this is definitely freezing."

"Below freezing, actually. Twenty degrees to be exact." He shut the door behind her. "You can have a seat on that stool by the counter, if you'd like."

A huge chunk of ice rested on a table. "As you can see, I've already drawn out a design on this. I use a special kind of chalk that contains ammonia and penetrates the ice."

"But how did you get a block of ice that size?"

A wry grin spread over his face. "This is an ice company, remember?" He chuckled. "We make ice here. See those two machines over there? They're working to make ice right now. They freeze the ice from the bottom up while water is circulating through. That keeps the air bubbles out, keeps the ice for sculptures from becoming cloudy. Takes three to four days."

"Wow. How much does that chunk on the table weigh?"

"The machine creates three-hundred-pound

blocks. For a large sculpture like what I'm working on today, I have to fuse the blocks together. First I cut them to the right size for the sculpture I have in mind, then sand them to a smooth surface. Then to fuse them, that's done by heating up an aluminum sheet and what amounts to ironing them. The chunk on the table is just over five hundred pounds."

Jessie strode to a desk and opened a small box then moved back to Casey and held out his palm. In it lay two small foam cylinders.

"What are these?"

"Earplugs."

Confused, Casey lifted the earplugs and wondered why she would need them. She watched Jesse, admiring his form as he marched to the other side of the refrigerated room.

He glanced over at her and pointed to his ears, then to Casey's surprise, he lifted a chain saw.

SIX

Inside the refrigerated room, Casey sat on a stool and shivered, despite Jesse's jacket and the knit cap and gloves she now wore.

She glanced at the clock on the wall. Eleven? Her stomach already growled like a man-eating tiger. She wasn't sure she would make it all the way to lunch. Hopefully, the guy would break for one.

Jesse held the chain saw high in the air and squeezed the throttle, revving the motor. She had the strong impression that he did that for her benefit.

He sent a mischievous smile her direction, confirming her instincts—he was showing off.

A smile slipped onto her lips as she took a sip of her coffee, what she now thought of as Jesse's signature brew. She'd need to top it off again soon because it was fast growing cold. She would definitely have had her fill of caffeine by the day's end. Unfortunately, that could lead to another sleepless night.

Jessie pressed the chain saw against the ice, sending a plume of frozen water into the air. She had the feeling he enjoyed the feel of power in his hands. Watching Jesse grind away at the ice with the chain saw, she couldn't ask very many questions at this juncture. So, she sat back and enjoyed watching the ice take shape under his careful and expertly placed cuts.

She'd have to figure out how to get her hands on a camera—this deserved to be photographed. Danny would expect the images, too.

As ideas began to grab her, questions for her interview began to fill her head. Casey leaned on the desk and began writing about what she saw and experienced—all the emotions that Jesse's artistry invoked in her, little by little.

Casey enjoyed slipping back into her role as a reporter working on an article, albeit a human interest piece, as opposed to an exposé. But Jesse's broad shoulders and masculine stance as he worked the chain saw were quickly becoming a distraction, invoking altogether different emotions.

Looking at Casey, Jesse allowed the chain saw to idle. "Right now," he said, raising his voice above the tool's noisome cadence, "I'm cutting out the main form with the chain saw, then everything else is removed with various-size chisels."

Casey smiled and nodded, taking notes like a good little reporter, trying to focus on the ice rather than the sculptor. At that moment, she realized she should have spent time learning more about Jessie

Dufour. Though she had nothing to compare his artistry to, his confident stance and the fruit of his labor bore witness to his ability and talent.

Her fingers growing stiff, despite the gloves Jesse let her borrow, Casey couldn't write anymore. She dropped the pencil on the pad and stood to stretch and get her blood circulation going again.

The racket of the chain saw suddenly stopped, and Casey glanced up to see Jesse staring.

"You're cold," he said, matter-of-factly.

She didn't want him to stop, but she couldn't deny the truth. "I'm not accustomed to sitting around in twenty degrees all day."

Jesse placed the chain saw on the floor and, when he approached Casey, she imagined how warm she'd feel if his arms were around her. But no, he simply tugged on her sleeve.

"Let's get you out of here."

She allowed him to guide her to the door, his hand near the small of her back. Once she stepped through the doorway into his office, she drew in what she hoped would be a breath of warm air. "I'm not sure it feels any warmer outside your freezer. I was starting to feel like a slab of beef in there."

Jesse laughed and took off his cap and gloves. "It's noon already. Did you need anything else from me?"

A sliver of disappointment lodged in her throat. Was he so anxious to get rid of her? Casey frowned, not caring that he saw. Admittedly, she was enjoying Jesse's company a little too much. She felt safe while she was with him.

"Actually, I need another cup of your coffee." Casey strolled over to pour some more. "And, I need answers. That wasn't exactly an interview. Plus, the newspaper wants me to follow you through the competition. Something for the front page, or at least the entire spread of the culture or entertainment section. Come on, then you'd get some publicity. Your picture on the front of the paper, especially if you win."

A deep crease grew in Jesse's brow and he stared at her as though he'd rather take a trip to a war zone. The man who gaped at her now was the old Jesse, not the thoughtful Jesse who'd saved her from an armed attacker in the house, or who'd changed her tire.

What had she done to create that change in him?

Growing warm, Jesse yanked off his hoodie, giving himself a chance to reply. Appearing on the front page of a newspaper was the last thing he needed in the middle of an undercover assignment. An article using his fake name was one thing, pictures were another. Still, he'd cleaned up his appearance from his last assignment near the Arizona border, so it wasn't likely he'd be recognized, especially wearing his knit cap.

Once the hoodie was off, Casey walked toward

him, a teasing smile on her lips. Jesse froze as she reached for him.

What was she doing?

With a soft laugh, she brushed her fingers through his hair. "Just needed a little grooming, that's all."

He closed his eyes. Her touch knocked him like a shockwave. He turned his back to her and tossed the hoodie over a chair. It landed on the floor instead. She was putting him off his game. He gave a huff and walked over to pick up the hoodie. Turning on his heel, he began busying himself in the room.

"Well? You haven't answered me. You said you'd give me an interview, but I haven't had the chance to actually ask you questions, have I? Can I watch you through the entire process? I won't be in your hair the entire time, if that's what's bothering you."

This operation was difficult as it was, maintaining the cover of an ice sculptor as he worked his way deep to learn who the players in the crime ring were. *That* was his real job.

On the other hand, he'd already decided he needed to keep her close. But her presence was clouding up the ice. He couldn't think clearly with her near. "It's complicated," he said.

She shrugged, and with a lilt to her voice, said, "I can do complicated."

Cute. Very cute. Jesse dropped his head and squeezed his eyes shut. "I believe you on that, but I'm not sure you can do cold."

Keeping her around here could be dangerous for

her. On the other hand, she didn't appear to have any inkling about what was going on, criminally speaking. That could be good, meaning she hadn't stirred any trouble with her sudden appearance and unmonitored exploration before Jesse had found her lost on the loading dock. Or he could be wrong—she could know very well what was going on and be using him to get into the ice company. Either way, Jesse needed to keep a close watch on her—because if someone in the crime ring had targeted her, Jesse would have to protect her.

Still, he was torn about what was the best way to keep Casey safe. She was an investigative reporter who claimed to be writing a human-interest story under the name Carson Williams.

"I'm pretty busy. Mind if I give it some thought?"

Though he hadn't meant his response as a commitment, she smiled like she'd won a Pulitzer. "I can learn to do cold. But I can't learn to do without lunch. How about I buy and you answer a few questions."

Phew, boy. Jesse ran his hand through his hair, wondering at the look she gave him. Did she detect he was already twisting under her scrutiny? No way did he want to be under the spotlight. But he'd done this to himself. "Sure, but I can't take long, because I have a few things to take care of this afternoon."

Like delivering the tire and finding out what really happened this morning. Discovering who Harrison Spear was, and when the next cash delivery would take place. He had his work cut out for him, and he hadn't even counted the sculpture competition.

He still had to maintain the appearance of being the company ice sculptor, which meant doing all the work involved and creating high-quality sculptures for the competition.

Jesse suggested they eat at a small out-of-the-way place he frequented. He had a few questions for her, too, like what she was really after. He hoped she was only going for the ice sculpting story. But, given her background, he needed to be cautious. They placed their orders, and Casey excused herself, heading to the restroom.

While she was away, Jesse checked his messages. Nothing. He intended to deliver her tire to forensics, but couldn't very well do that with her tagging along.

A few minutes later, Casey slid into the booth across from him. She tugged a recording device from the same bag Jesse had confiscated from Carlos and Miguel only yesterday.

He was liking this less and less by the minute. "Uh, do we have to record our conversation?"

She frowned. "I guess not. It's not the kind of reporting I usually..."

The waitress approached their table, carrying a bowl of soup for Casey and an Italian sub for Jesse. After she left, Casey offered to say grace. Jesse bowed his head, thinking about how long it had been since he'd heard someone bless a meal. It felt nice.

Though Jesse struggled with moral issues regarding his career choice and reconciling that with his Christian life—the things he'd done in the name of his job—he'd reached out only this morning, begging God to keep Casey safe. And God had answered that prayer, hadn't He?

It was a start.

She slurped her soup then looked embarrassed. "Sorry."

Jesse smiled. "That's okay. You'll forgive me if I happen to drop sauce on my shirt, won't you?"

She laughed. He liked the sound, and to see this side of her, rather than the fear in her eyes, the tears and the trembling he'd experienced from her over the last day or so. Jesse's throat constricted.

"Since I don't have much time, what say you ask me questions while we eat?" he asked.

"I have a million and this could take days. First, where did you get your training? What is your background?"

A bite of Jesse's sub lodged in his throat. He grabbed his water to wash it down. These were the exact kind of questions he hoped to avoid, but what had he expected?

"I created a few pieces in college for fun. Entered competitions. I guess you could say I just have a knack for this sort of thing." Of course, he left out that his dad was a master chef, and Jesse had learned from him, but that information could jeopardize his mission. He'd given her as much truth as he could.

If he didn't play this just right, his supervisor, McCoffey, was going to have his neck—he might anyway. Jesse admitted he'd grossly miscalculated where this path would take him when he agreed to her interview to begin with. But he'd had his reasons then, and he supposed those reasons still remained—to keep an eye on her. But, would Mc-Coffey agree?

"College. Did you major in culinary arts then? Where did you attend?" Casey scribbled on her pad.

Jesse's cell rang. He glanced at the ID.

McCoffey. "I've gotta take this call, sorry. Hold on."

He slipped from the booth.

He was aware that Casey watched him, even as he walked out the front door. The phone call had given him a reprieve from her questions that had taken a personal direction. Somehow, he needed to direct the interview back to his current occupation, the ice-sculpting process, and the upcoming event.

If only they could have met under different circumstances. Fortunately, since he was using an undercover name, she wouldn't be able to discover anything about him on the internet, except what she could find about him on the company website.

But that could prove to be a problem, as well, if she became curious about his past. A fake background planted on the internet just for her benefit would mean lies upon more lies. Jesse wasn't sure he could stomach much more.

"What's up?" he asked, letting McCoffey know he was able to talk.

"Harrison Spear's story is not holding up—he doesn't appear to have any connection to John Helms as a family friend. But he's been seen talking to David Gussy. There could be a connection there."

David Gussy was second-in-command to John Helms. "And the flash drive that Spear dropped?"

"The computer-analysis recovery team is on it. I'll let you know when I know."

"And the girl?" Jesse already knew she was an investigative reporter.

"She's a reporter with a history—easy to track. She quit her job in Oregon about a week ago. It's unclear why she left, but it appears she drove straight to Southern California to John Helms's house."

"To an empty house." But why? Certainly not to see relatives. Jesse didn't bother telling McCoffey she was interviewing him. That would not go over well. He'd find out soon enough.

"Stay focused, Jesse. She's a distraction. Nothing more."

Jesse ended the call and headed back into the restaurant.

At their table, he noticed Casey's bowl of soup

was gone and a cup of coffee took its place. "You're still not warm?"

"Guess not. But no worries, it's decaf," she said, and tugged her pen and pad out again.

"Listen, I'm sorry, but something's come up, so I can't finish the interview right now."

"What about later this evening?"

Jesse didn't answer. What would it take to get her completely out of the picture? McCoffey was right, she was an interruption to this operation, a distraction.

"Look, I really need this story. You see, I don't have a job if I don't interview you."

Was she serious? He needed to weasel his way into hanging out with Miguel this afternoon. He was doing double duty as it was.

"Can you meet me at the studio at seven? I've got plenty of work left to do on that sculpture."

"But I need to talk to you, ask you questions. Your noisy tool doesn't lend itself well to interviews."

"I promise, by then, I'll be using the chisel, and we can talk while I work." He was an idiot.

Jesse glanced out the window and watched a silver SUV drive by the restaurant. He left Casey sitting in the booth and ran past the tables and booths filled with patrons. An elderly couple shuffled through the front door just as Jesse needed to push through, the bell announcing their arrival.

Jesse eased by them but short of knocking them over, he couldn't exit the door fast enough.

The vehicle was gone. How many of that make and model could there be in this town? Could the drive-by have been sheer coincidence? Jesse pulled out his cell. He intended to find out.

SEVEN

That afternoon, Casey sat at a makeshift desk in a forgotten cubicle that Danny Garcia had offered and began working on what little she had on the interview. It was very little, but it had been enough to convince Danny that she had an article. She chewed on her pencil and stared at the computer screen, her fingers on the keyboard.

That is, it was enough if Jesse didn't wig out on agreeing to meet her tonight. What was with him anyway? One minute he was coming to her rescue and fighting off villains, changing her tire, all while being attentive to her needs and sprinkling that with a little flirting. The next minute he acted like he wished he could scrape her off his shoe. It was enough to drive a reporter looking for a story crazy. Desperation had driven her to seek him out in the first place, and then extreme situations had driven her to experience safety in his arms. The powerful attraction she had to the man didn't help matters.

But Jesse's protective nature seemed only to

appear under the direst of circumstances. She'd completed an internet search on one Jesse Dufour and came up with no one by the same name who fit, except for a cursory mention on the Helms Ice website. Jesse was a conundrum. She'd have to work harder to shove aside her incessant need to dig at the truth. She wasn't a truth finder now, she was a fluff reporter.

Get in for the story and get out. That's all you need to do.

She'd needed this job for the money and something to take her mind from Will Tannin, but maybe it was a mistake to ignore what happened this morning. Casey reached for her phone, planning to call Meg and find out if Tannin was still in Oregon.

Danny Garcia appeared in the cubicle entry, his wavy black hair nearly covering his left eye, and a pencil shoved over his ear. He tossed some papers on the desk. "Here. Fill these out. You can't get a paycheck until we have your info. It's all contingent on the story. Don't forget."

Casey's throat tightened. "I got it."

He slid to partially sit on her desk. "What exactly brings you to our little town, Miss Wilkes? I read some of your work. You're good."

Casey rolled her chair back and studied Danny. Was he friend or foe? A little twinkle in his eye told her the former. "Just call me Carson, okay?"

Danny laughed, revealing his other side. He wasn't so gruff, after all. Or maybe it was just that all the men in Orange Crossings had to appear tough and unlikable at first.

"Carson it is." He slid off the desk and walked out of the cubicle as though he'd given up his inquisition, but then, at the last second he leaned back in. "Just so we're clear, when things have died down and you're willing to write a real story, let's have a go at those exposés. That is, if you're planning to stay."

Casey felt her jaw drop.

"Don't look so surprised. I talked to Eddie and he explained. What? Did you think I wouldn't check up on you?" Danny smiled then disappeared.

He knew? He'd talked to Eddie? Then why did he ask? Did that mean Eddie wasn't expecting her to come back?

A quiver started in her belly then worked its way over her body. She hoped Danny's call to Eddie hadn't somehow been intercepted by Tannin, or could somehow lead him to her. She'd been flabbergasted at the lengths to which he'd gone as it was—the email and newspaper hacks.

Oh, Danny…why couldn't he have simply asked her instead? He'd taken her on her word that she could get the story, and he hadn't exactly inquired about the details of her résumé.

She'd thought this morning's incident could have been more of Tannin torturing her because he'd found her. Then she'd dismissed it. Jesse's questions had made her believe she was overreacting, but she was reevaluating the wisdom in that.

Jesse.

He'd been there, protecting her both last night and this morning. But she'd be a fool to think she could count on him to be there every time, especially if Tannin did show up. Jesse wasn't her protector, for crying out loud. He wasn't even her boyfriend, nor did he have a clue she was in danger, that she'd been running. She barely knew the guy and yet she'd allowed herself, if only for a short time, to take shelter in his arms.

By five o'clock, Casey had some semblance of an article, though she had plenty of empty space in her outline of questions. After shutting the desktop computer down for the day, she blew out a breath and shoved to her feet. It felt good to be back at work. She'd drive through Taco Bell before swinging home to grab something warm to wear. Tonight she'd wear her own coat, so she wouldn't have to endure Jesse's scent, though she hardly found it distasteful. But that was beside the point.

She wondered which Jesse she would get—the Jesse who sent warm tickles through her or the Jesse who made her think she was an annoying fly he wanted to swat.

That had to be it. He didn't like reporters.

Her cell rang. *Meg.* She'd been waiting on this call.

"Hey, girl. Got your message."

"Well?"

"Will Tannin is still in town. I did a drive-by and spotted him with that same woman. Who knows? Maybe they're an item now."

"Do you think he's forgotten about me? Forgotten about his threats?"

"I think it's too soon to know. You haven't been gone that long. And remember, Casey, you destroyed his life. That's something he's not likely to forget anytime soon or ever."

Having handed off Casey's tire for further investigation, Jesse sped through town, hoping he didn't miss her. When he turned into the parking lot of the ice company, he found her leaning against her car, waiting. Fortunately, he'd had a chance to mention to Miguel and Carlos that Casey was interviewing him, and he'd be working with her tonight at his studio. He was treading too close to the brink, but there was no going back. Admiring her slim frame, Jesse pulled into a parking spot a few spaces over.

When he climbed from the Jeep and made his way around, she shoved upright from the car and smiled. "I was afraid you'd forgotten."

"Nope, didn't forget," he said as he tugged the keys to his studio out of his pocket.

Unlocking the door, he held it open for her. She strolled in, a jacket slung over her shoulder.

He liked her spunk. "I see you remembered to bring a coat."

She whirled around and smiled at him. "Yep. I've got all the necessities for a night out in the cold, except maybe a bag of chestnuts." She tugged a cap from the coat pocket.

"Chestnuts?" Jesse closed the door behind him and locked it since it was after hours.

"You know—'The Christmas Song'?" Casey sang a few lyrics of the old classic. She had a good, strong singing voice.

"Hey, I wouldn't have thought you could sing," he teased.

She sidled up to him as he started making coffee. What was she up to? Flirting to see if she could get more answers from him? Well, he was on to her.

"What's that supposed to mean?" she asked.

"It means I didn't know reporters could sing."

She slung her bag at him. Laughing, he ducked, almost losing the coffee grounds. "Hey, watch it. You want coffee or not?" What was it about this woman?

"Actually, I'm buzzing from too much already."

"Well, if you want some, I'm making it for you." He stuck the carafe into the slot and turned on the switch. When he looked at Casey, she had an expression on her face that he couldn't place. Soft and glowing and…questioning. She had the look of a woman who wanted more than an interview.

Jesse kept his hands to himself, firmly planted in his pockets. But his gaze left her eyes—that couldn't be longing he saw there, could it?—and traveled to her lips. Was she toying with him?

Thinking of McCoffey breathing down his neck, Jesse frowned. He had work to do, and Casey was getting in his way. Miguel was close to giving him what he needed to finish this operation. That's all he wanted.

"Ah, now don't do that," she whispered.

"Do what?" He crossed his arms and leaned against the counter. His suspicions were beginning to mount. She was using her sweet tone to play him. To his chagrin, he admitted it might, just might, be working.

"Don't switch back to the old Jesse."

"The old Jesse? I think you've had too much caffeine, like you said. You're not making any sense." He shoved away from the counter and walked toward his office. Placing his hand on the doorknob, he swung around to look at her. "You ready?"

She nodded. He tried to ignore her graceful, feminine movements as she strolled his way. *Get a grip, man.*

"I like the other Jesse, the guy who's nice to me, who changes my tires and smiles in a warm, friendly way."

Oh, that Jesse. The one who'd slipped and subtly responded to an insane attraction to her. The one who, if he allowed that part of him to respond to her again, just might give too much away in the interview. That had to be what she was after.

Casey was a sharp woman and had read him well. He'd better stay on his toes while near her.

He held the door as she stepped through and tugged on the jacket she brought. "You are one moody man."

And here he thought he was doing a bang-up job of managing his roles.

Mesmerized, Casey had watched Jesse work with his chisel, bringing the block of ice to life. For just over an hour she had asked him questions about his background—which he managed to generalize— and about ice sculpting. Her fingers were getting numb again so she put aside her notepad.

"You know, I think I might be able to figure out what you're carving."

"Oh? What's that?" he said, without looking at her.

Still, she saw the grin on his face.

"Something Egyptian—like a throne of some sort."

"I'll never tell. I'm not sure it's going to be enough for the competition."

"I think it's beautiful."

For the first time since she'd started talking, he paused. He stood tall and stretched his arms. "I'm glad you like it," he said.

He'd answered her questions satisfactorily, at least well enough for her to write an article. Except, she had one more.

"Have you decided yet whether you'll allow me to follow your progress through the competition?"

Jesse chipped away at the sculpture again, ignoring her question. She knew he'd heard her. He'd been listening and answering questions for a while now. What could she do to convince him to let her stay?

He seemed to like her for more than just a reporter—at times, that is. But then, he acted as though he wished she would just leave. Why couldn't he be one way or the other? It would make things much easier.

Finally, he stood and tossed his chisel on the table. "I didn't realize it was so late and you're cold again. Your lips look blue."

Casey reflexively put a gloved finger to her mouth. She glanced at Jesse and noticed his gaze lingered on her lips. "You're right. We should call it a night. I'll come back tomorrow."

He blew out a breath, appearing drained. She wondered what sort of strain an ice sculptor would come under doing his job, but then his stress could have everything to do with family or other circumstances and nothing to do with the job. But so far, he'd managed to evade all her personal questions except for one.

She'd ask him about a significant other and he'd shaken his head. She'd breathed a little easier knowing their innocent flirting, when it arose, wasn't intruding on a relationship.

Casey wanted to know the real Jesse Dufour. Not just the ice sculptor. How did she break that barrier? How did they become more than a reporter interviewing a sculptor?

"Listen, I told you I needed to think about it. Give me until tomorrow, okay? But have you gotten what you need for your article? So you can get your job?" This time he poured on the double-dimple grin.

Casey slipped and nearly fell off the stool. She was tired, that's all. "I think so, but I'm hoping for more."

Their eyes locked, and Casey couldn't bring herself to look away. Jesse didn't fare any better.

"I need to go," she said. She'd seen something behind his eyes—it terrified her and thrilled her at the same time.

"Yeah, wait up, and I'll walk you out."

Casey pushed through the door into the warmer room, though it was still too cool for comfort in her opinion. At least she was able to accomplish a lot today and could be proud of this article when she finished. Hopefully, Danny would like her work and allow her to continue to work with Jesse through the competition.

The only roadblock now was Jesse, himself.

Fifteen minutes later, he still hadn't come out of that freezer where he carved the sculptures. Maybe he needed to pack it away for the night or something, though she couldn't see why.

What was he doing in there?

Casey opened the door to look inside, hoping to hurry him along. On the phone, he jerked his head up and knitted his brow. Hadn't he said he wanted to walk her out? Too tired to deal with his mood changes, she slammed the door.

"Goodbye, Jesse Dufour," she whispered and hurried out to the parking lot. The door closed automatically behind her. Suddenly Casey was startled by the dark. What happened to the lights?

The minimal illumination from distant parking lots didn't help her much, and clouds must have moved in, hiding the moon. She couldn't see a thing, much less her car.

It was a little creepy out here.

Casey reached behind her for the door handle and tugged.

Locked.

Okay, there was nothing for it. She had to go forward. Picturing where she knew her car to be, she moved in that direction but tripped on something, bending her ankle at an awkward position.

Casey yelped. She stepped on her foot again to test it. She'd live.

Feeling somewhat embarrassed at her outcry—though who would have heard her—and her sudden fear of the dark, Casey stood perfectly still and took a deep breath.

There. Nothing to worry about.

Footsteps sent her heart racing.

Somewhere in the parking lot, athletic shoes scraped the concrete.

Casey gave a nervous laugh, hoping to dial down her fear. "Have you got a flashlight?"

No answer. The footfalls drew near.

"Who's there?"

EIGHT

Fear kept Casey paralyzed. *Come on, come on, run... Lord, help me!*

Had Tannin finally found her? Or was she simply overreacting?

The door had to be closer to her than her car. Besides, she'd have to unlock it and right now, it could take her too long to fumble for her keys. Casey broke from the stranglehold of fear and stumbled back to the door.

She pounded on the door, not caring if she looked like an idiot. This could be nothing, after all. Then again, the prickles on her arms told her danger approached.

Bang, bang, bang. "Jesse, let me in!"

The footfalls grew quicker. Whoever was in the parking lot was coming directly toward her.

She turned to face her assailant, flattening herself against the door and praying Jesse would open it in time. Still, she saw nothing, no one, in the darkness.

Casey's knees trembled, and she worried she might slide to the ground.

What a helpless weakling and coward she was. Drawing from somewhere deep inside, she braced herself.

Fight if you have to. Fight!

Casey placed her large bag in front of her, wishing she'd carried a weapon inside. Even something heavy like a hand weight would transform her purse into a deadly weapon. She'd thought of that weeks ago because of Tannin, but then believed she'd escaped him.

A whimper broke from her throat.

Behind the door, a sound infused her with hope. The door pushed open, shoving her forward. Light from inside the building illuminated a strip of the parking lot.

A man stood a few yards away.

Casey screamed.

He slipped into the darkness—gone as though he were a figment of her imagination.

Jesse tugged her inside, closing the door behind them.

He gripped her shoulders, piercing her with his gaze. "Casey, what happened? Are you all right?"

A sob escaped as she shook her head, unable to answer. Heart pounding, she pressed her face into his shoulder, and he slipped his arms around her, comforting her. She didn't want to grow accustomed to this.

And what did Jesse think was going on with her? If she didn't tell him about Will Tannin, he was going to think she was crazy now for sure.

Finally, she gained control over her emotions and stepped back. Sniffing, she slid a hand under her runny nose, wishing she had a tissue. "That man, did you see him?"

"Yes. Did he try to hurt you?"

"No, I mean...I thought..." What did she think exactly? "It was dark and I heard someone walking toward me. I asked who it was, and he didn't answer. That's when I pounded on the door for you to let me back in. Jesse, the door was locked, for crying out loud."

Jesse studied her, looking a little like he wasn't sure he believed her. "Are you sure that he wasn't just a bum making his way across the parking lot?"

Casey found her way to the cushy chair and slumped into it. She shoved her hands over her face. "No, I'm not sure."

She blew out a breath, disturbing a strand of hair that had fallen over her left eye.

When Jesse said nothing, Casey continued.

"It's just that, I felt like whoever was out there was coming for me. I know he was walking toward me, and then he walked faster when I got to the door. Why was your door locked?"

She wondered if and when Jesse would ask her why she was paranoid. Ask her about her past or if she had a reason to believe someone would want to harm her. But…he didn't.

The guy was an ice sculptor, not a cop or even an investigative reporter. What did she expect from him?

He stared at her, concern in his eyes. "Did you get a good look at him?"

Casey closed her eyes, trying to focus on the image burned there. "No, he looked like any other guy. Average everything." Except for…his eyes. But what could she say? She'd only seen the guy in the light for a millisecond. Still trembling, she shoved from the chair. She had to lose her fear if she was going home tonight.

"Why didn't you wait for me?" Jesse unplugged the coffeemaker. He turned off the lights in the back of the room and grabbed his hoodie and a flashlight. Then he slipped something off the counter.

"I…you were on the phone."

He quirked a brow at her and tugged the hoodie over his head. "You're impatient, you know that? Here. Now you have a key."

Casey looked at the small key in his hand and hesitated.

"Go ahead. I could be using the chain saw and in that case, I'd never hear you knocking."

She could always go through the reception area. Nah. Casey took the key. "I promise to give it back as soon as I'm done with the story. Um…thanks."

Jesse nodded and pressed past her to the door.

"Are we…? Are we going back out there?"

Smiling, he closed the distance between them and rubbed her shoulders. "You're trembling," he said, his smile flattening.

The tenderness in his voice nearly made Casey forget about the scare. Why couldn't she ignore the way he affected her? She nodded, unsure what to say or do because she didn't want to go back outside. Not yet.

"Don't worry. You're with me now. I'll protect you."

Could he really? "With what? Your flashlight?"

Jesse held up the big Maglite. "You'd be amazed at what harm can be inflicted with one of these."

"You're serious?"

"Trust me, will you?" He lowered the lights and whispered in the darkness. "Stay right behind me."

Casey clung to the back of Jesse's hoodie as he opened the door and stood in the doorway, shining the flashlight around the unlit parking lot.

"Is it usually so dark out? What's wrong with those lights?"

Jesse moved forward, Casey with him, and allowed the door to close behind them. "Maybe a tripped circuit. I don't know."

For someone who didn't seem to believe Casey had reason to fear the parking lot stalker, Jesse's muscles were tense as she pressed her hand into his back.

* * *

Confident the man who scared Casey was long gone, Jesse escorted her to her car and waited for her to start it. "Go ahead. I'll be right behind you."

She gave a little nod and a tenuous smile. "Thanks, Jesse. I appreciate this."

Jesse suspected he was days away from the next smuggling transaction. All players were preparing on both sides—agents and local authorities on the side of the law, and those in the crime ring.

While he was relieved that Casey didn't press the matter, his sense of unease regarding her safety was mounting. He tried not to appear overly concerned, hoping his manner would keep her from full-blown panic.

Jesse followed Casey's car along Shoreline Road as fog began drifting in. Headlights appeared in the distance, driving toward them. Tension coursed through his body as he waited and watched, but the vehicle passed without incident.

Casey was on edge and with her experiences last night, this morning and now tonight, she had good reason. She pulled into the driveway and waited while the garage door opened.

Jesse kept his Jeep running and the lights on while she pulled the car in. He hopped out and followed her into the garage just as the door began to close. She turned on the garage light.

He looked around, impressed with the spotless

surroundings. Usually, people had all sorts of junk stored in their garage. "All clear," he said.

She nudged him with her bag and smiled. "Coming in?" she asked, as she made her way to the door of the house.

Good. She'd relaxed some. Jesse stepped inside, his senses on alert. Without any discussion, he helped her turn on all the lights and walked through the house with her, similar to what he'd done the night before to make sure there wasn't a man lurking in the shadows.

Like Spear. Would he come back to search for his missing thumb drive?

Jesse's gut instinct told him that this woman had lived in a world of fear long before coming to Orange Crossings, and he'd bet she left her job because of it.

What or who are you running from, Casey Wilkes?

Standing in the foyer, Jesse knew he didn't want to leave. Casey rubbed her arms and leaned against the wall. He could tell she wasn't looking forward to being alone.

"Listen, I have an answer for you," he said.

She quirked a brow. "What was the question?"

"Forget already? Well, in that case..." Jesse turned to open the door.

If only she'd forgotten her request, then Jesse could be done with the interview and concentrate on his assignment. But she'd remember soon enough, and besides, after three close calls, no way was Jesse going to abandon her.

He needed to keep her close because by all appearances, someone was out to get her, and if that was the case, his worst fears were coming true.

Casey was at his side, her hand on his arm. Again, the shock of her touch coursed through him.

"No, wait. Please, what's your answer?" she asked, her voice a soft whisper. The sound of it tied him in knots. Why, oh, why, did he have to be attracted to a woman he needed to protect?

Jesse swallowed, shoving down his rising desire. He cupped her chin but then just as quickly released it. "You can tag along with me for the next few days for your story. That is, if you still want to."

Her answering smile sent his heart stumbling. Her lips were inviting as she lifted her face and held it mere inches from his.

Jesse pressed closer, drawing in the scent of her. Her breath came faster.

What are you doing, man?

For her sake and for his, he cleared his throat and took a step back.

"I'll look into the mysterious man in the parking lot for you." And he would, but she had no idea just how much danger she could be in...or did she? The sooner he found out what was going on, the better.

"Thanks." Casey smiled, but he could see the disappointment in her eyes. Frustration he keenly felt himself.

Or…on second thought…

He studied her. Maybe what he was seeing was a frightened and vulnerable woman who needed a distraction. Then again, he'd sensed she was attracted to him before tonight. But in his line of work, he couldn't mix business and pleasure.

That could mean the end of him.

"Good night," Jesse said and stepped outside. As he waited, listening to the telltale sound of the dead bolt, he ground his teeth. He'd practically had to wrench himself away from her, from kissing her. With a weighty sigh, he scanned the yard and decided to check the perimeter.

Somehow he needed to accelerate this operation, before someone else got hurt.

NINE

After a morning of working with the ice, Jesse shoved open the door and strode into the parking lot, welcoming the warmth from the sun on his face and knowing that soon enough his chilled body would begin to thaw.

Jamming his hands in his pockets to warm them, he walked the perimeter of the building and turned the corner, making his way to the loading dock. A refrigerated semi was backed up to the entrance, preparing for long-haul ice deliveries.

As he approached, the familiar noise of the trailer doors being slammed and fastened resounded. The truck jerked with a rumble and slowly moved forward, pulling away from the loading dock.

Miguel stepped into view and hopped from the ledge. He spotted Jesse and waved him over. Jesse grinned. The more time he could spend with Miguel the better. Desperately, he needed in the circle. Too bad he couldn't have gotten a job driving a truck to begin with instead of working as an ice sculptor. It had made his mission even more difficult—yet, he'd come this far. Still, driving wouldn't keep him at the ice company to make the contacts he needed.

Carlos stood at the dropoff and scowled when he saw Jesse. He turned his back to him.

Likewise, dude, likewise.

Where he'd scored points with Miguel, even being called his brother, he'd lost them with Carlos. The man could be the reason Jesse wasn't pulled completely into the crime ring.

Carlos was standing in the way.

Jesse approached Miguel and stood next to him, watching as Miguel took a drag of his cigarette.

"What are you doing outside? Did you get too cold?" Miguel asked, a familiar wry grin on his face.

"Something like that," Jesse said, and returned the smile. The guy really liked him, Jesse knew that. It made him feel all the worse for the charade he played.

To hide his traitorous thoughts, he looked away from Miguel.

There, leaning against a light pole in the distance, stood the same guy he'd seen last night, scaring Casey. Jesse was sure of it because the guy hadn't bothered to change his clothes. He wore the same maroon hoodie and worn jeans. Though Jesse had only gotten a glimpse of the guy previously, it was enough to recognize the guy who was loitering now as the very same one.

"That's him," Jesse said and left Miguel's side, stalking toward the man.

"Hey, Jesse, where you going?" Miguel called. "Who is he?"

"Some guy who threatened Casey last night." Jesse marched toward the man, knowing that Miguel and most likely even Carlos would be watching this encounter.

Miguel snickered. "So, you got a girlfriend now." His tone was teasing. Jesse didn't respond. He couldn't exactly question the guy in front of them at least what he really needed to ask him— that would blow his cover. Seeing the guy and doing nothing about him would likely raise their suspicions. He needed to respond in a natural way— one that Miguel and Carlos would understand.

Even from this distance, Jesse could see the guy's squint and the very instant he realized Jesse was coming for him.

Good.

The guy straightened, shoving away from the light pole as he tossed his cigarette down. His stance told Jesse he was bracing himself for a confrontation.

Even better.

And it told Jesse a little more about him—he was military. Marine, maybe?

Jesse was ready for the confrontation, too. The guy's actions alone went a long way to confirm to Jesse that he hadn't just scared Casey because he was at the wrong place at the wrong time. He'd intended to do harm.

Had he been expecting her today?

Once Jesse stood directly in front of him, he poked his finger in the man's chest. "Who are you? What do you want?"

The guy flipped opened a switchblade—by the look of it, old German style, white Macarta handle.

Jesse laughed. "You call that a knife?"

The man snarled. "Your girlfriend was scared of it."

Jesse didn't remember a knife, nor had Casey mentioned one.

But that remark was all it took. Before the guy could react, Jesse grabbed his wrist and twisted his arm behind his back.

He threw himself into a forceful head-butt. The knife clattered to the ground. The man threw a punch at Jesse, who took that as an invitation to do more damage. He was on the guy in full force, landing blows to his gut.

The guy shoved his fist into Jesse's nose. Adrenaline kept the pain at bay. Jesse shoved the flat of his hand in an upward motion at the jerk's nose. Jesse looked on as the guy's eyes watered.

Still, the guy managed a smirk as he stared at Jesse.

Unbelievable.

Then he turned and, scraping his knife up, ran

away. Maybe he thought Jesse would simply let him go, but Jesse followed and caught him. Pinning him down, Jesse lifted his fist with every intention of pummeling him senseless.

What are you doing, man? Jesse didn't want to seriously injure this man, but he'd just broken his nose and could have killed him with that move. The guy was strong and knew how to fight, too. Things could easily turn his way, could easily get even more out of hand.

Jesse eased back and drew in a breath. He couldn't allow his anger to get the best of him. He drew in a quick breath, planning to ask the man who had sent him.

A shadow fell over him.

"You all right?" Miguel asked.

"Yeah, I got this," Jesse said. Then to the hoodlum, he warned, "If you ever show your face here again, I'll kill you."

Jesse released him, though he didn't want to. The man scrambled to his feet then took off. The look on Miguel's face said it all. Jesse's pulse had begun to slow, if only a little, but now it raced again. This could be exactly what Jesse needed to prove himself, get points for being a tough guy. That is, if he played things just right.

Miguel's expression was one of amusement and concern. He squeezed Jesse's shoulder. "You don't look so good."

After dragging in a few more calming breaths, the adrenaline receded and Jesse felt the pain in his face. His nose throbbed, and his eye was swelling.

Together, he and Miguel walked back to the loading dock where Carlos stood with a big smile on his face.

It was the first time Jesse could remember seeing a look of approval from Carlos. Jesse had earned Carlos's respect for beating up the guy. He would use this, play it for everything.

"You're such a tough guy, why didn't you just kill him?" Carlos asked.

Blood dripped onto the floor, and Jesse realized his nose was bleeding. He shoved past Carlos. "Too lazy. Didn't want to clean up the mess," he called over his shoulder.

Carlos and Miguel followed him from a distance as he made his way through the loading dock, toward the entrance into the building. He could use the sink in his studio to clean up.

"Sounds like you have some experience," Carlos said, a challenge in his tone.

"I do." Jesse glanced over his shoulder, then he opened the door and walked out.

And he did. As an agent, he'd taken the life of another human being in self-defense. Carlos didn't need to know the particulars. It was enough for him to know that Jesse would and could kill.

Maybe now, Jesse would be worthy.

* * *

Casey's eyelids drooped as she stared at her laptop. Since she'd fled from Oregon, it seemed like she'd run from one stressful situation to another and hadn't had a chance to recuperate from the initial shock of Tannin's threat. At this rate, she wondered if she ever would, and the strain was wearing on her.

Dressed in sweats, she'd made herself comfortable on the sofa as she watched a news program and dug into research on the new story Danny had given her. It was a good sign, and showed his confidence in her abilities.

She was thankful he wanted her to continue her work on the sculpting story and upcoming competition. She was looking forward to seeing Jesse again tomorrow.

Noting that it was already nine o'clock, she sighed. She hadn't seen Jesse today, but a day not spent in his company had probably been for the best. Where Casey was concerned, the man was habit-forming. Every time she turned around she was in his arms. While she found a measure of peace and safety there, she wasn't sure it was in her best interest, or his. Jesse had no idea Casey had driven a man to threaten her life and that man was potentially searching for her right now.

Every time she considered telling Jesse, she decided against it. The story was difficult to believe, and she didn't want to sound crazy. In a way she was trying to start a new life here, at least until things died down. Did she want to spoil her chance to start over, to start fresh, by telling Jesse? No. At least not yet. Maybe the time would come, though, when she would feel comfortable sharing that with him.

Please, Lord, let me find a safe harbor, a place where I no longer have to worry about Will Tannin's threat.

And a time when she would no longer have to fear for her life. A person couldn't imagine what a driving force that could be until experiencing it. She certainly hadn't. And yet, she'd brought it on herself to some extent.

But as Meg had said, Tannin was still in Oregon and, at least for the time being, she hoped he hadn't found her. While she tried to push aside the incidents of the past two days as merely coincidental, it was almost impossible. She couldn't let her guard slip and she remained cautious and on edge—something she was sure Jesse had noticed about her, hence his questioning her reaction to the man in the parking lot, and to the SUV's intent at harming her. Still, despite what he might or might not have believed, he'd proven himself a protector, watching out for her.

Someone knocked on the door.

The sound startled her. Her senses ramped into high gear. Who could be knocking at this hour? It was late for a house call, especially without phoning first.

Wary, Casey crawled from her comfortable position on the sofa. She didn't really know anyone in town, except Danny, Jesse and a few coworkers she'd met today. When her aunt and uncle returned, Aunt Leann would probably introduce Casey to her friends.

Cautiously, she crept to the door and gazed through the peephole.

Jesse!

Relief and excitement slammed her cagey emotions like a riptide. She unbolted the door and tugged it open, unable to help the smile spreading over her face. "What a surprise."

Uh-huh. Hadn't she just been thinking a day away from him was a good thing?

Barely aware of the alarm beeping in the background, Casey soaked in Jesse's bad-boy good looks. Were all ice sculptors this gorgeous? Did they all have to be muscular and in shape to handle chain saws? Or the sheer weight of huge blocks of ice?

He shoved a hand through his hair and kept Simon, who wagged his tail in delight, from leaping on her. "I was…in the neighborhood," he said, with that double-dimpled grin.

What more could a woman want? Except Casey wasn't in the market for love; she was in hiding for her life. The reminder almost dampened her enthusiasm at seeing Jesse. For the moment, though, she ignored the reality of her thoughts.

She opened the door wide. "Come in." She gave the alarm system the code it needed to shut down for the time being. Aunt Leann had given her instructions for resetting the code, thank goodness. No more friendly intruders.

Jesse stepped into the foyer, still holding Simon. "I came to ask if you would like to go for a walk on the beach."

When the light fell on him she gasped. His eye was red and swollen. "Oh, Jesse! What happened?"

He chuckled and lifted a hand to his eye. "This? It's nothing."

"You have a shiner. Did you get in a fight?"

"Sometimes I have to wrestle with a stubborn block of ice. Nothing that won't go away in a few days. It'll probably be gone tomorrow."

Casey wanted to run her finger around the edges of his swollen eye, but kept her hands to herself. "I'm sorry. I know that must hurt."

Suddenly, she remembered she wore raggedy sweats and looked down at her appearance. "Oh, well, *this* is embarrassing."

He laughed. "I'm sorry I didn't call first, but it's all right. All you need is a jacket and besides, I don't mind your appearance one bit."

His gaze drifted over her.

He's flirting again. "Just let me grab one." Casey dashed off to the bedroom for a sweatshirt and wondered how long he'd stay in his current mood. She hated to think about how much she liked being with him.

She tugged the sweatshirt on and, just because she couldn't stand the thought of him seeing her in her comfy but ratty sweats, she pulled on a pair of her favorite jeans and her tennis shoes. In the bathroom, she tugged her hair into a ponytail and brushed her teeth.

There. At least she was presentable. But she was definitely insane for letting Jesse affect her like this.

Casey hurried from the bedroom and, glancing out the panoramic window at the ocean, spotted Jesse on the deck. She slipped out to join him. "You ready?"

"Yeah…" Jesse glimpsed her way, then swung his gaze back to her where it lingered. "I think there's a storm brewing in the distance. We might not have much time."

Lightning flashed on the horizon in the distance, confirming his words.

Simon pawed her, and she leaned over to pet him. "You're such a good boy," she said. She adored Simon and had the feeling she could easily grow to adore Jesse, too.

If she already hadn't.

Jesse led the way down the steps of the deck and onto the beach, and soon they were striding side by side, a full moon highlighted by a hazy ring lighting their way. A salty breeze caressed Casey's skin and whipped a few loose strands over her face. For the first time Casey could remember, she couldn't think of anything at all to say, as though a schoolgirl crush had tied her tongue into knots.

Still, it was a comfortable silence. Jesse had stopped by to see her and it had nothing to do with her story, nor was she in imminent danger. But she warned herself not to jump to conclusions. He could have stopped by to check on her, considering that she tended to attract trouble.

Jesse released Simon from the leash and the dog took off across the beach, barking.

"He sounds happy, if you can tell that by a dog's bark," Casey said with a chuckle.

Jesse laughed but said nothing.

"You're a mysterious man, Jesse Dufour." Casey wasn't sure why she'd so easily voiced her private thoughts about him. The next thing she knew, she'd be telling him everything about her life in Oregon, and about Tannin.

"Why do you say that?"

"Because I can't find out anything about you, about your past." That fact disturbed her. "I'm supposed to be dong a story on you, remember?"

Simon came bounding back, carrying a piece of driftwood. Jesse took it from the dog and tossed it. Somewhere in the distance, thunder rumbled. Maybe the storm would pass them by.

Suddenly, Jesse turned to face her and stepped

into her space. "Is that all I am to you, Casey Wilkes, a story?"

A knot lodged in Casey's throat. He was close, oh, so close. His cologne swirled around her. She closed her eyes, remembering the almost-kiss last night.

His lips were on hers, sending warmth through her entire body. She melted against him, lost to the world around her.

He'd become much more than a habit for her. He was an addiction.

TEN

Jesse ended the kiss and pressed his nose against Casey's, holding her hands in his. He sighed. "I'm sorry, I shouldn't have done that."

"No. It's okay," she said, her words a little shaky. Then a playful grin tickled the corner of her mouth. "I liked it."

Could she be any more appealing?

"And," she added, "you're more than just a story to me."

"Are you sure?" he asked.

"I'm sure," she whispered.

He wanted more than anything to believe it. But did he really? She could be playing him because she was after a different story all together.

Wasn't Jesse playing her?

He was a man torn in too many directions. He'd kissed her to keep her from asking questions. He'd kissed her because he wanted to kiss her. And now, where did that leave the both of them?

Him acting out a part, and her falling for *that* guy, not the real Jesse.

She didn't have a clue. And he was a jerk for it.

From the beginning, he'd wanted to prevent anyone else from getting hurt or, worse, killed, at the ice company. He feared Casey was in danger, but where would she be safest? With him? Or far away from here? It wasn't within his power to send her away. Not without the threat of discovery.

For those reasons and a million more, he was torn over how best to protect Casey.

And worse, he was falling for her.

Help me, God. What do I do?

She lingered against him, her breath smelling minty, like she'd just brushed. He smiled a little at the thought. All the chaos in his head melted away as he savored this moment with her.

Thunder clapped, too close for comfort, startling Casey. She jumped and he wrapped his arms around her.

He'd thought it before—she was a woman on edge. But why? "The storm's moving in fast. Maybe we should get back."

Simon returned just in time and, barking, ran ahead of them toward the house.

"I don't want to get caught in the storm. Race you!" Casey took off running. Surprised, Jesse laughed and then gladly followed. He had every intention of letting her think she was winning until the very last second.

Casey glanced behind her, shooting a mischievous smile at him. Keep that up and she'd lose without any effort on his part. Jesse burst forward and tagged her. She stumbled, and he fell next to her, laughing. A drop of rain smacked him in the face.

Lying in the sand next to the deck, Jesse looked up and noticed the lights were out. Footsteps pounded the sand, running from the house.

Simon growled and barked, then ran in the direction Jesse had heard the footsteps come from.

"That wasn't a happy bark." Casey sat up. "Jesse?"

Jesse jumped up. "Stay there!" He ran after what he feared to be another intruder. Had they armed the system when they left? He didn't think so.

Idiot!

Large raindrops began pelting him and, with the clouds moving in, the moonlight was no longer lighting his way. "Simon!"

The dog barked somewhere in the distance. Jesse paused and considered giving up on catching whoever had run from the house and began to worry about leaving Casey alone. Simon could find his way back.

From somewhere ahead on the dark and stormy beach, Simon yapped in pain. The sound crushed Jesse, angered him.

Should he go back for his standard company issue SIG P226 locked safely in his car?

An arm gripped his biceps. Fist raised, he turned and almost slammed Casey.

Lightning flashed, revealing that she was soaked to the bone. "I told you to stay put," he yelled over the storm.

"I was too scared, so I ran after you."

A few yards away, Simon limped toward them, whimpering.

Casey knelt down, "You poor thing."

"Come on," Jesse said, and lifted his dog.

"And be sure to arm the alarm system and lock the doors this time, ma'am," Officer Perry said, standing in the doorway.

"Thank you for coming. I will." She smiled and shut the door when he left.

Casey was glad when he'd finally turned off the flashing lights—they had to be disturbing the neighbors, especially at this hour. Then again, those same lights were certainly a deterrent to wannabe intruders.

What was going on?

She leaned against the door, pressing a trembling hand to her forehead, and blew out a breath. "What a night."

She'd called the police to inform them of a possible intruder, and she suspected the only reason they sent a cruiser out was because it was John Helms's home. But again, she felt like an idiot. Nothing was missing—at least that she knew of. Jesse suspected they had scared the person off before they could enter the house.

"You've got to be exhausted." Jesse stood with his legs wide apart and arms crossed, watching her. He had to be concerned about his dog.

"Listen, you can go now. I'll be fine, really. This is just a bad neighborhood, I guess." Her laugh was insincere as she plopped on the sofa next to Simon. Resting comfortably, he lifted his head slightly to look at her, then rested it against his paws. He'd come back to them, limping, but he seemed to be better now.

She ran her hands through his fur, enjoying the feel of it, and knowing she brought him comfort, as well. For some odd reason, she didn't believe the intruder—or alleged intruder—had anything to do with Tannin. It just...wasn't his style.

A shudder ran through her at the thought—maybe he'd done damage after all, or left something she wouldn't discover until later. Absurd—he was in Oregon State, nearly a thousand miles from here.

Keep telling yourself that.

That should bring her relief, and she'd thought by staying in Aunt Leann's home, she'd feel safe. But that wasn't the case at all. Maybe her uncle's company had something to do with the attacks.

There was something to Jesse's odd behavior, and the cell-phone guy she'd first encountered at the ice company but then later dismissed.

She was staying in the owner's house, after all. When she looked at Jesse, she wondered what he had to do with it, if anything. Suspicion splintered through her again.

He held her gaze, concern and something else in his eyes that almost took her breath away, washing away her errant thought. She couldn't bring herself to believe anything bad about Jesse right now.

She lifted a hand to him, an invitation for him to sit next to her. He answered, slipping his hand into hers, except he sat on the edge of the sofa, leaving a few inches between them. Though his action disappointed her, she reminded herself how he affected her—for his part, he'd made a wise decision. She wondered if he'd kept distance between them for the same reason.

She needed to focus on something else.

"I haven't exactly been in town long enough to find a church. Do you have any suggestions?" she asked, running her hand around Simon's ear.

Jesse's eyes narrowed, if only slightly, making her wish she hadn't asked. His reaction hurt because she cared for him.

"Where did that come from?" he asked, his voice sounding strained.

"Oh, I don't know. I need help getting through… whatever this is."

A tenuous smile replaced his frown. "We can find one together."

That wasn't exactly the answer she was hoping for—that he hadn't already been attending somewhere—but she'd take it. "I'd like that."

He smiled and looked at the coffee table. "If you think you're going to be all right, I need to leave now."

What is going on, Jesse? She desperately wanted to know. But Jesse didn't have the answers. "Sure, I'll be fine. But what about Simon? Are you going to take him to the vet tomorrow?"

"His leg will be fine. Whatever happened, he's not limping anymore. If you don't mind, I was thinking of leaving him here—that is, for you, to keep you safe."

"Don't you think that's overkill? Especially if I set the alarm?" she asked, a tremor in her voice. She knew enough about alarms to know they weren't foolproof, even when set. If someone really wanted in…

"Whoever was here is long gone, and with the cops coming out to look around, I doubt they'll come back. But there's no better protection than a guard dog, though I wouldn't exactly call Simon ferocious. Still, he can protect you."

Casey's throat constricted. Maybe she should just move out of her uncle's house. But how? She'd need money to get an apartment or rental home. And she was already in a lease in Oregon—she'd paid for the next three months up front. Where, then, could she go?

Besides, her initial intention was to wait things out where Tannin was concerned. She hadn't considered how long that might take when she'd decided to run.

"Thank you for your offer, but no, I'd feel guilty having Simon here—he'd miss you. Plus, I'd be responsible for him. I can hardly take care of myself as it is. Isn't that obvious?"

"It's your decision, of course." Jesse called Simon to him, then just before he stepped outside, he turned back to her. "Don't forget what the sergeant said."

"I got it. Set the alarm."

Still. Would it be enough?

Jesse dropped Simon off at his house and headed back to watch Casey. He hadn't known how to respond to her comment regarding taking care of herself. It wasn't as if he could spill any of his concerns because they were all related to his mission.

All evening, he'd wondered if Spear had been the intruder. Had the guy returned to look for the thumb drive? If Casey had been home would he have simply knocked, and questioned her politely? Or had he been waiting for her to leave?

His pulse thrummed in his neck. What if…what if he had planned to question her in a similar manner to the way he'd handled her the other night, and then he'd taken off when he'd seen Jesse with her?

Argh. There was so much Jesse just didn't know, so much information that he was still waiting on—like how many silver SUVs were in the area? Had

Casey's tire been tampered with? Was there anything relevant on that thumb drive? Anything incriminating? Or was Spear telling the truth?

These things took time, and they distracted him from his real focus—the sting operation to bring down the cash-smuggling crime ring.

Pulling up next to the curb and behind a van a little distance from the Helmses' home, he prepared to keep vigil, watching over the house. It would have been nice if Casey had allowed Simon to stay—that way Jesse could have stayed, too, though outside, and without her knowledge. Instead, he'd had to take Simon home. The dog had whimpered a little when he jumped from the Jeep, his leg still bothering him. Jesse suspected whomever Simon had chased had kicked the dog, but he didn't want to say so in front of Casey, increasing an already stressful situation.

Nevertheless, he knew Simon would be fine. If his pain persisted tomorrow, Jesse might take him to the vet.

He settled back in his seat. Before he could get too comfortable he needed to make sure that she was still all right, that everything was status quo since he'd left her.

He called her and held his cell to his ear, the house in full view from where he sat.

"Jesse?" she answered on the first ring. "What's wrong?"

"Does there have to be something wrong for me to call you?" Definitely on edge. He almost chuckled when he considered how often their time together had been a result of something going wrong. But it was anything except funny.

"Uh, no. It's just late, that's all." She sounded tense, rather than groggy.

"I'm sorry if I woke you," he said. "I wanted to make sure that you were all right."

"As in, has someone else tried to run me over or break into the house or get me in the dark or if I'm scared to death to be alone? No, you didn't wake me."

Whoa. "Now that was a mouthful. I take it that no one has bothered you, but how are you doing? Mentally, that is?"

She sighed, and this time he heard drowsiness slipping into her voice. "I'm scared, Jesse. And I'm so exhausted, I'm not sure that my fear can keep me awake. How's that for an answer?"

"You're going to be fine tonight, Casey. Get some rest."

Another sigh resounded over the line—one of contentment. She was settling, then. The sound stirred something deep inside Jesse. He laid his head against the headrest and closed his eyes. Maybe he would just stay connected with her, on the phone, all night, or at least until she fell asleep.

"Do you believe in God, Jesse?"

Jesse squeezed his eyes. All the questions she asked relating to God—like earlier tonight about church were tough. If she had any idea how far he'd been from God, the things he'd done in the name of his job...

"Yes," he said. It was all he could manage.

"Pray for me then. Pray for me that God will watch over me."

Oh, he'd prayed for her already—it was because of her that he'd put aside his own fears of approaching the Almighty and sent up a prayer for her safety.

"I will."

"Good night, Jesse Dufour."

The rain started again somewhere around three in the morning. He didn't know whether to be glad for more rain—because it might be a deterrent to criminals—or not, because it was limiting his vision of her house.

He'd contacted McCoffey to ask for help in watching Casey, because he couldn't watch her all the time and continue with his cover. He had half expected an earful regarding his involvement with the reporter and how she could cause him to blow everything he'd worked for, and he got it. If anyone discovered her shadow, though her escort should be invisible even to her, the entire operation could be in jeopardy.

Jesse had ground his teeth and pressed his back against the seat, enduring the tongue-lashing. Nevertheless, Casey had an answer to her prayer— someone to watch over her. An agent was being assigned to her and would watch from a distance starting tomorrow morning.

Eventually, when his raging pulse had subsided, Jesse fought to keep the steady rain from lulling him to sleep.

Casey lay in bed, unable to sleep. With the storm passing through, the night was dark except when lightning flashed, illuminating the guest bedroom where she slept but casting long shadows with each strike. Finally, she'd turned on the bathroom light rather than fear the dark like a child, but her dread of the darkness had nothing at all to do with non-existent monsters.

The light only provided a little comfort and if anything, kept her from falling asleep, she finally decided. She kicked off the covers and got up to switch the light off, her mind a jumble of chaotic thoughts about why she was even here, the strange incidents that occurred the last three days and about Jesse.

He was a conundrum to be sure, and she wasn't absolutely one hundred percent convinced that he was someone she should trust— especially given the extraordinary circumstances. But...

He'd confessed tonight that he wanted more from her.

He wanted to mean more to her than just another interview, and in this situation, for Casey, just another job. And Casey felt the same way. Hadn't she been trying to figure out how to take their acquaintance—barely a friendship—to the next level? Meg would accuse her of moving too fast. Casey had chided herself, too, for her thoughts about Jesse. He didn't know about Will Tannin. He didn't know that Casey was in hiding and that she might have to leave again and quickly. He didn't know her new life was a lie.

But when you had that long-awaited connection with someone—why not acknowledge it? Rolling to her side, Casey punched the pillow to get more comfortable. What could be better than a guy you really liked, liking you back?

The thunder and lightning finally grew distant and rain drummed against the window, soothing her to sleep.

Her cell rang, startling her awake. Heart pounding, Casey reached over to the side table. Late calls were never good news. Unless…did Jesse miss her? Was he calling again?

She was crazy.

"Hello?"

Silence and then…

Breathing, heavy breathing…

Casey tensed, paralyzed once again.

She threw the phone across the room and it smashed against the wall. Casey tossed the covers off and got up to get the phone and remove the battery. Once she got back in bed, the momentary adrenaline dissipated leaving Casey with nothing but fear. She stuck her face in the pillow and sobbed. Will Tannin had gotten her phone number. How long would it be before he found her?

A twinge of pain shot up Jesse's neck. He jerked awake. He squirmed in the uncomfortable seat and rubbed his hand over his face, trying to come fully awake. With the approaching dawn, the skies began to clear, and would leave behind the gift of a warm and humid spring day.

A glance at the clock, and he realized he'd slept for only half an hour. Considering someone had been in the house last night, Jesse wanted to watch Casey until she made it to work today, until her watchdog arrived.

Jesse hoped he'd remain secure behind the van so Casey wouldn't notice him. She shouldn't be driving right past him on her way into town. He also hoped she'd leave before the neighbors got up, but knew he was leaving a lot to chance.

Two hours later, he watched the garage door to the Helmses' home rise and a little green car back from the drive. The car shot up the road in the direction of the newspaper offices. Jesse pulled out from his hiding place and followed from a distance. This wouldn't take too long.

Just make sure she gets to work.

Her escort would pick it up from there. Jesse could run home and grab a quick shower before heading to the ice company.

But Casey drove right past the newspaper.

ELEVEN

Casey passed the *Orange Crossings Times* where she should have headed first. Danny liked to have meetings in the morning and he'd invited her to attend—she was becoming part of the newspaper crew.

She glanced into the rearview mirror, looking at the circles under her eyes and then back to the road. Her palms were slippery against the steering wheel as she turned into a shopping-center parking lot.

Since Casey had trashed her phone, she needed to buy a new one. She didn't want to wait another minute, knowing that Tannin had her number. How had he gotten it?

The only reason she'd purchased a disposable phone was that she'd heard they were supposed to be untraceable. Right. She should get her facts straight next time.

She had called two people in Oregon from the phone—Meg and Eddie—to let them know she wouldn't be back until it was over. Had those calls been a mistake?

What else did Tannin have?

Her new address?

How far away did she have to go to be free of him? Had she known he would take things this far, she would never had written the article.

Scratch that. She would have anyway. And if she had any fortitude in her at all, she'd see this through to the end.

And win.

But right now, she needed a new phone and she needed to finish the ice-sculpture story and she needed…

To stay alive.

Her thoughts jumped to Jesse. After all of this was over, would she have a future with him? She hurried into the store and purchased a new phone, paying cash—a resource she was running out of and too quickly. Back in her car, she transferred the numbers she'd saved from her old phone. A silver SUV pulled into the parking lot.

An image of the same vehicle driving straight for her blazed through her mind, sending her pulse racing. Casey started her VW, uncertain if it would be better to simply run back into the store and call for help from there.

The vehicle parked, and out jumped a woman and two children. Casey pressed her forehead against the steering wheel. How long could she live this way—in a constant state of fear?

For a minute, she allowed herself to imagine what it had felt like to be in Jesse's protective arms, and her heart ached.

Would he still be interested in her once he knew about her exposés? What she'd done to someone else's life, regardless of their guilt? And that that someone was after her?

Casey focused on completing the transfer of numbers.

She got out of her car and strategically placed the old phone under her tire. The act reminded her she needed to have her spare replaced. Did Jesse have the new tire yet? But one thing at a time. Then, she drove over the phone, crushing it—dramatic, but it made her feel good all the same.

There, Will Tannin. Let's see how long it takes you to track me down again.

She shuddered at the thought. If she received another harassing phone call any time soon, she'd have to make some changes and fast.

Driving through the parking lot, she spotted the nose of a Jeep—with a suspiciously familiar bent license plate—protruding from the corner of a building on the far side of the shopping center.

Jesse...

Should she drive over and say hello? She slowed for a moment to think, but considering she didn't know what business he was on, she decided it might be awkward. Besides, she was late to work at a job she hadn't really secured yet.

Way to go.

She looked forward to the moment when she would see him again today, but she had to stop by the newspaper first. As she continued out of the parking lot, she glanced in her rearview mirror and saw the Jeep nudge forward slowly.

She exited the parking lot and took a right, planning to head back to the newspaper, though she wondered if that was the best idea, given her state of mind.

Frazzled didn't come close to describing how she felt. But she was trying to hold it together. As she made her way down the road, then took a left onto Main Street, she spotted Jesse switching lanes five cars back, and she realized that he was following her.

What else could it be?

She'd had a thousand miles of practice on her drive from Oregon to become accustomed to watching for a tail. And she didn't like it.

Not one bit.

It felt too much like being stalked, even by Jesse.

Casey swung a sharp right, plunging into a dark alley, and waited. She climbed out of the car and leaned against it, arms crossed. If he was following her, he'd be here soon enough. He'd want to know why she hadn't come back out—it was a dead end.

But why was she reacting like this? How many

times had he been there for her? Had she considered him as a protector? Her determination began to melt—what if Jesse was simply trying to protect her now?

If that were the case, then he must think she was in danger, and she hadn't been a paranoid fool all this time. Then why didn't he say so?

Hyperventilating, Casey put her hands over her face. She honestly didn't know which end was up. She really was losing it.

When she let her hands drop, Jesse stood in front of her.

"*What*...are you doing?" he asked.

Casey stared back at him, dark circles accenting the wild look in her eyes. Her hair looked a little tousled as well. It scared him.

"What am I doing? What are *you* doing?" she asked, vehemence in her voice he hadn't heard before that moment.

He was seriously concerned. The girl was cracking under the pressure.

Jesse held his palms out and opened his mouth to explain, "I—"

"Why are you following me?" she snapped, suspicion in her eyes.

"If—"

"Who do you think you are, anyway?"

That was it, Jesse had had it. He reached out to

grip her shoulders, but she shrugged him off and backed away. "Casey, calm down," he said.

Her chest rose and fell with the fury of the moment, her eyes ablaze.

"Just…calm down, will you? You're scaring me."

Her breathing slowed, and she looked away from him, tugging her hair behind her ears.

Like all the other moments he'd pulled her into his arms to comfort her, he wanted to do the same right now, but he sensed she wouldn't allow it.

Her eyes glistened and she blinked the tears away. Jesse had the feeling she'd had enough, and was done with the tears. She'd been more than aware of his tail, which told him she'd had practice in looking for one.

"Why are you so upset?"

Folding her arms across her chest, she rubbed them and shook her head.

Again that niggling feeling, gut instinct this time, Jesse had no doubt.

Casey was running. "Who is following you, Casey? Who are you running from?"

"No one," she said, a wild look still in her eyes.

"You're lying."

"Why were you following me, tell me that?"

Jesse hated to admit he hadn't been prepared for this confrontation. "I…uh—" he lifted his shoulders "—you know why," he said, then let his shoulders drop.

Her eyes seemed to clear as though her thoughts

had, as well. "No, I don't. Why don't you tell me what's going on? Why would you want or need to follow me?"

"You've had a few close calls. I just wanted to make sure you were all right."

He honestly didn't know what was going on. He planned to have dinner at Miguel's tonight and see if he could find something out. But if Casey were running from someone before she even arrived in Orange Crossings…

"I'm sorry, Jesse. Sorry for blowing up at you."

"Now, maybe you can tell me why you're so upset."

Casey released a ragged breath and tried for a smile. "I think I'm just tired. It's like you said, so many close calls. They've left me wondering what will happen next. And then when I saw you—"

"But that doesn't explain why you lost it like that."

Her eyes widened at his words.

"Casey, has someone been harassing you? Has someone followed you before? Stalked you? Tell me." *Maybe I can help.*

Just thinking of her possible answer sent Jesse's blood to the boiling point.

Suddenly, a silhouette appeared at the alley's opening. Jesse tensed and reached around his back for the gun he'd holstered out of sight.

The silhouette morphed into a man, and once he

realized the alley wasn't empty, he skulked away. Jesse allowed himself to relax a little.

"Uh, mind if we take this conversation somewhere else?" He guided her to her car, opened the door for her to climb in, and then got in the passenger side. The VW wasn't exactly his preferred mode of transportation, especially with his knees taking up half the front seat, but he'd parked his Jeep in the street.

Still appearing a little too haggard for comfort, Casey looked over at him. "Don't you have to carve ice today?"

"At some point, yes."

Casey turned the car around in the small space and drove from the alley. "You know, I really need to get to my new job."

"So tell the editor you're working, interviewing me. You don't have the job without me, do you?"

"Funny thing, that, but...you're right." She phoned the newspaper with her new phone and explained that Jesse's schedule required that she spend more time with him this morning.

Casey drove down a side street while Jesse directed her. "Over there, park over there. See the swings?"

"What, no coffee shop or back street dives?"

Jesse didn't laugh. "What we have to talk about is too important. I just didn't want us to stay in the alley."

Casey did as he asked and they left the car and strolled on the sidewalk around the small city park. Though she'd calmed since laying into Jesse, she still wasn't sure she wanted to have this conversation with him. What would he think? Would he even want to finish his interview with her if he knew the kind of reporting she'd done?

Seagulls fought over breadcrumbs in the park as a salty ocean breeze wafted over Casey—the usual, peaceful scene one could see in any small town nestled against the ocean. Except Casey wasn't exactly feeling the peaceful vibes.

"Are you going to tell me what's going on or do I have to drag it out of you?" he asked.

"No, Jesse, I don't want to tell you."

Jesse stopped and stared at her. The hurt in his eyes surprised her.

"Why not?"

Casey had been startled that he'd read her so well—how had he known that she'd been harassed and stalked? Maybe that was fodder for another story the victims of stalkers who lived their lives in fear. She sensed he wanted to protect her, and, drawn to him, she couldn't deny she needed and wanted his protection.

She wanted to feel safe. Blowing out a breath, she searched Jesse's eyes. He was the man who had made her feel safe, and even now, she was glad he was here.

"All right, but you're not going to like it. I asked

for the trouble I'm in, and you're probably not going to like me anymore after I tell you."

"Who says I like you?" Jesse winked and grabbed her hand, holding it in his.

He was teasing, she knew, trying to soothe her.

For some reason, the action reminded her of his kiss last night and how all the fun of the evening had been interrupted, ruined, by an intruder.

If only her affection for him wasn't overshadowed by her fear. She hated what Tannin was doing to her life. And in a way, she finally understood what she'd done to him—though she was sure he never feared she would kill him.

And with the thought, she drew in a shaky breath. "I wrote an exposé about someone in Oregon—a man named Will Tannin. It started out innocently. I wanted to know why and how he could justify making so much money while working for a charity, a non-profit. One thing led to another, and I discovered he'd done a few things he shouldn't have."

Jesse studied her, his patient gaze waiting for her to continue. A couple strolled past and Casey waited until they were out of earshot. She and Jesse continued their walk around the park.

"Now that I think about it, maybe he wasn't really a criminal, or hadn't had criminal intent, but made a few mistakes. Like sleeping with a woman he was supposed to be helping through the charity." Casey watched a seagull fly overhead then looked back to the ground. "In the end, my article destroyed his life, and because he lost everything, I think he lost his mind. Add to that I learned that he'd gotten help in the past for some sort of psycho behavior—he was an abusive person, had stalked someone. Jesse, it's not good that now he blames me for everything."

"And now he wants to destroy your life."

"He's done a pretty good job of that already. Now he wants to kill me. He grabbed me from behind one day and told me how he would kill me using words so foul and violent." Casey shivered and wrapped her arms around herself. "He planned to make me suffer first. I don't know why he let me go, but that's the day I left Oregon and tried to hide."

Jesse stopped their stroll and released her hand. He grabbed her shoulders and turned her to face him completely, his face inches from hers. "You listen to me. If this Will Tannin so much as touches a hair on your head I'll—"

"You'll what? What will you do, Jesse?" Casey took a step back, shaking her head. She hated the tears pressing behind her eyes. "You can't protect me."

"Casey, I *will* protect you. You're safe with me." The passion in his voice and concern written across his face almost convinced Casey. At least he believed it himself.

And maybe…maybe he could protect her.

"There's something else, and it's probably the reason I reacted to you so fiercely today."

"What is it?" Jesse's voice sounded hoarse with emotion.

"He called again last night."

TWELVE

He called again last night....

Casey's words from earlier in the day continued to squeeze Jesse's chest like a vise, creating so much pressure he thought he might explode.

Jesse hadn't been able to let go of those words since he heard them, even while driving to Miguel's home that evening. He needed to mentally prepare for tonight. He hadn't seen Miguel or Carlos since leaving them with the suggestion that he'd killed someone—the truth wrapped neatly in a made-to-order package meant to entice.

But hearing from Casey that a man wanted to kill her, and she'd fled her home to hide here in Orange Crossings? Jesse had expected something, but not that. Here he'd been trying to keep her safe, and she was already embroiled in danger.

McCoffey didn't want to hear about it—it wasn't Jesse's problem, and he'd blasted him, stating Jesse needed to focus on his assignment. But he couldn't exactly do it all—spy on the loading-dock guys, work his way into their circle, create ice sculptures as part of his cover and watch over Casey.

Jesse had made sure Eric, Casey's invisible tail who'd finally made a show, knew about this new threat, or rather old threat, and that Casey was adept in watching for shadows.

He almost chuckled at the thought of Casey pulling the alley stunt on Eric like she had on him, but it was a serious matter. If she discovered Eric, the agent sent to watch her, then Jesse's identity could be compromised. Casey would want to know everything.

He wished he could share the truth with her—that he was working undercover. How much easier it would make things for the both of them, that is, if she wasn't a reporter. Because she was an investigative reporter, the truth could cause more problems than it solved. She was disrupting his life as it was.

Though Jesse had every intention of keeping Casey close while she worked on her story and he worked through this operation, he was somewhat relieved that her editor had asked her to come in this afternoon. Jesse needed time to digest the information she'd shared—he needed time to see if there was anything he could do about Will Tannin.

One thing he still didn't know. Were the parking-lot lurker and the intruder related to Casey's stalker, or instead connected with the cash-smuggling operation? If God was willing, Jesse would learn the answer to that tonight.

Already late for supper, Jesse drove through the suburban sprawl where Miguel lived, but before he reached Miguel's house, his cell rang. Jesse drove right past Miguel's house so that he could give the call his full attention.

"Jesse, this is Dallas." Dallas Comer was a member of CART, or the Computer Analysis Recovery Team. "You've hit pay dirt, man."

Jesse had sent the thumb drive he'd discovered the night of his scuffle with Spear back to headquarters to be analyzed. "Yeah?"

"I'll send you a copy of the report, if you want, but McCoffey already has it."

Dallas explained that the disk contained incriminating information regarding the ring. Computer forensics would need to confirm, but they believed that Spear could have tried to plant the information onto John Helms's computer.

They were getting closer, but to secure the convictions they needed, the key to Jesse's mission was to witness the bulk-cash-smuggling transaction.

The sooner he could bring this to a close the better, especially where Casey was concerned.

Pressure squeezed Jesse's neck and shoulders — he had to succeed, but success came with a price....

Finally, Jesse stood on the porch to Miguel's home and raised his hand but didn't knock. He squeezed his eyes shut, imagining Elena, Miguel's wife, spitting in his face when her husband was arrested all because of Jesse. He had no doubt that she would, once this was over.

The door opened and Rosita, Miguel's six-year-old daughter, stared up at him, batting her long, dark eyelashes. One day, she'd grow into a beautiful young woman. While she might have a crush on him now, if Jesse were successful, she'd hate him for putting her daddy away.

"Hi, Mister Jesse."

Grinning, he squatted to eye level and cuffed her on the chin. "Hello, Miss Rosita."

She giggled and ran away, leaving the door open. Miguel came forward and extended his hand to grab Jesse, pulling him completely into his home, tugging him into a bear hug, a brotherly hug. "You're late."

Jesse smiled, returning the familial affections. He liked Miguel, loved his family. But the guy had made some bad choices. Jesse grinned when Elena entered the room and flashed her gorgeous smile.

"Little Rosita is going to be as beautiful as you one day," Jesse said, feeling as if she was his sister.

"Ah, Jesse, you're such a flirt." She came over and squeezed his cheek like his grandmother used to. "A flirt that needs a wife or at least a girlfriend that can make sure you are on time to supper. I made your favorite, but you're late, and now it's cold. I'll dish some up for you."

He thought about the call he'd taken on the way to Miguel's house. His heart ached for what he would do to this family, for tearing it apart. But Miguel was the one to blame.

Then the irony hit him—both he and Miguel were living double lives on opposite sides of the law.

His smile faded as he focused again on his mission, the reason he was here. To infiltrate, to bury himself deep within. Unfortunately, that often meant getting involved with the family.

"I'm very sorry. I got held up. Did Miguel leave any dessert for me?"

Miguel punched his arm. "Elena has been fighting me off for the last hour."

Jesse followed him into the dining room, where a chocolate cake waited in the middle of the table. A few dirty dishes still remained—remnants of what looked like cheese enchiladas.

Yep, his favorite.

Elena appeared in the dining room, holding a steaming plate of enchiladas. "You know how I hate to microwave food. Now the cheese is burnt and the tortillas are dried out."

"I'm sure it's still delicious." Jesse smiled, took a seat and ate his enchiladas then started on the cake. He drank serving upon serving of coffee as Elena offered, and enjoyed the banter of this family, all the while thinking of the reasons he was late.

"Tell me about your sister, Jesse. You mentioned her last time. Where does she live again?"

"Jersey. She's divorced, a single mother with two young children."

"That's always hard. I don't know how people do it," Elena said.

"I send her as much money as I can to help with the bills, but right now that's not much."

"Why don't you bring her here to live with you in California?" Miguel set down his cup of coffee and leaned back.

"It costs a lot of money to move someone across the country." And it was true. Jesse had tried repeatedly to convince Kathryn, but she refused his help—at least on that front, stating it was too much, and she wouldn't allow him to pay. What more could he do? He wondered if she had a romantic interest keeping her there.

Jesse rubbed the back of his neck while Elena removed his empty plate. "The cake was delicious."

"Thank you."

Miguel rose and motioned for Jesse to follow him. He shoved open the screen door. "It's nice tonight, like every night. I love it here."

When Miguel sat, Jesse did, too. Jesse prayed that Miguel would soon bring him in on his plans, allow Jesse to be a part of the business.

"That woman, the reporter, is she done?" Miguel asked.

Jesse tensed. The fact that Casey was on Miguel's radar wasn't a good sign. "No, she's working on a story about ice sculpting, focusing on me and then the competition through next week."

Miguel smiled, easing some of the tension from

Jesse. "There's a little light in your eyes when you talk about her. Like Elena says, you need a woman in your life. You like this reporter?"

Jesse's body temperature spiked a few degrees. Miguel shouldn't be able to read him so well. What did that say about his cover? "Looks like you're on to me," Jesse said, and grinned.

Miguel stared off into the distance as they listened to sounds of children playing, dogs barking and the occasional car passing in the neighborhood. No one would ever guess what Miguel was involved in.

Jesse waited, hoping and praying for something, anything from Miguel. When Miguel blew out a long breath, Jesse knew the man struggled with what he wanted to say.

"What is it?" Jesse asked. "Something's bothering you, my friend."

"You need extra money, and I need a driver. I've already run it by the boss. He asked if I could trust you."

Jesse held his breath.

"I can trust you, can't I, Jesse?"

Jesse didn't answer. It was an impossible question. Instead, he leaned forward, putting his elbows on his knees. "What do you want from me, Miguel?"

"I need you to make a delivery on ice, maybe more than one."

Good. Miguel hadn't pressed him on the point of trust, assuming his response was answer enough.

"Count me in." The words tasted like acid. "I'll be there for you."

"Aren't you curious about the deliveries?"

"None of my business." *Laundering money by smuggling it as cold hard cash.* "But if you think it's important that I know——"

"It could mean the difference between success and failure."

Jesse waited as Miguel studied him for a full thirty seconds, then, "Money, Jesse. We're delivering cash. And you and me? We get a cut of it."

"You can count on me to make sure the cash is delivered where it needs to go."

Miguel's mouth slowly curved into a grin. "I knew you were the man for the job. But there's one more thing. If you want your girlfriend safe, you need to keep her out of trouble. I know you like her, but be careful. She could be playing you, Jesse."

"Playing me?"

"Using you while she digs for another story."

Jesse couldn't believe what he was hearing. He squeezed his fist, wanting, needing to push things if only a little further. "Miguel…is she in danger?"

The man shoved to stand, bearing a more serious expression on his face than Jesse had ever seen on him. "Maybe."

It was what Jesse had feared all along…but still, hearing Miguel say the words were like a huge chunk of ice pressing down on him——he felt paralyzed under the weight of it. "Miguel, she's doing a story on the ice sculptures, that's all. I care about her. Help me out, will you?"

It felt strange—him reaching out to a member of an organized crime ring for mercy. He never dreamed that he would be reduced to this.

Casey strolled out of the movie theater and tossed her bag of popcorn into the trash. "Well, what did you think?" she asked.

"I loved it!" Tessa, a coworker from the newspaper had invited her along to a movie, and Casey had agreed, believing she needed a serious distraction from real life. Still, throughout the entire romantic comedy, Casey couldn't stop thinking about Jesse's words—that he would keep her safe.

"I'm glad you invited me. I've been a little stressed lately," Casey said.

"Yeah, me, too. Life can get so hectic. I wish I could meet a hunk like Matthew McConaughey, though."

They strolled out of the theater and into the parking lot. A light flickered off in the far corner, reminding Casey of the night when she'd stumbled into the dark and a creep had scared her. If Jesse hadn't opened the door, would the man have done more than simply scare her?

For weeks and months now, she'd prayed that God

would protect her. Could Jesse be the one He'd sent? But how could he help her?

As cars pulled away from the theater, Casey spotted someone leaning against her car. Tessa had parked next to her and they walked together.

Jesse. Her heart sprang into backflips. How had he found her?

"Who's that?" Tessa asked. "He's cute."

"Just a friend," Casey said, thinking about their friendship born of peculiar circumstances.

"Maybe you can set me up with him." She flashed Casey a smile.

Casey startled at the woman's words. "We'll see," she said, but considered Tessa's request for all of about two seconds.

When Casey was almost to her car, Jesse's smile grew wide, spreading into his double dimples.

She loved that smile.

Leaning against her car, with his arms crossed over his chest, and his shoulders appearing broad and powerful, he looked like a man who could definitely protect her. It felt good, more than good, to finally have shared what was going on in her life. Almost like he shared the weight of her burden with her.

"You went to a movie without inviting me?" Jesse asked. "I'm hurt."

Tessa gave a little wave from the other side of her car. "Good night, Casey. Maybe we can do this again," she said.

"Sounds good," Casey said. She watched Tessa climb into her car, then her gaze slid back to Jesse. "I didn't think you'd be interested. It was a chick flick."

He studied her. What was he thinking?

"Come here," he said, reaching out for her.

Casey flew into his arms. She had been thinking about him all day. "Is public display of affection against the law in Orange Crossings?" she asked, her words vibrating against his shirt.

"I'm all for getting arrested. How about you?"

She laughed, allowing herself to soak in the feeling of being in his arms, the feeling of being in his embrace.

"You weren't following me again, were you?" Even if he was, Casey decided she didn't mind.

"After everything you told me today, when you didn't answer your phone, I was worried," he said. "So I drove around. Your green bug is easy to spot."

Casey savored the timbre of his voice in his chest. "I needed the distraction. I'm sorry, I didn't think about it."

Jesse untangled himself from her and tipped her chin to look in her eyes. "No, the truth is you don't believe me. You don't think I can protect you."

"No, I didn't. But…I'm starting to." It felt good to know someone was actually trying to look out for her.

"Good." His intense gaze searched hers. "But you still need to be careful."

"What more can I do, Jesse? Are you saying I shouldn't go to the movies?"

"You might try having me as your escort next time."

Casey smiled. "I like that idea." Little by little, she was beginning to feel like everything would be all right—that Tannin wasn't going to find her, despite his phone call last night. One phone call didn't mean that he knew where to find her, did it?

Jesse ran his hand behind her ear and down her jawline. She pressed her cheek into his hand, wondering if he would kiss her.

"I'll follow you home," he finally said.

Casey drew in a ragged breath, trying to mask her disappointment. "You don't have to—"

"I know I don't, but it will make me feel better, knowing you're safely tucked away inside that house."

Casey only nodded, wondering why she'd ever questioned his offer to see her home, because the thought of Jesse taking on this role was all that was holding her together at the moment. She could fight this thing, especially with Jesse at her side. She refused to analyze it at the moment—she might end up deciding that Jesse was mistaken to believe he could help.

Once they were at her aunt's house, Jesse completed his walk-through—something else that was becoming a habit—to make sure there were no intruders. Casey couldn't help herself. She had to voice the thoughts that had been bothering her.

"I hope you understand now, why I've had such a knee-jerk reaction, thinking someone was trying to run me over, thinking the guy in the parking lot was out to get me."

Jesse studied her. "Of course I understand. And the fact that you spotted me following you says that you're staying aware of your surroundings. Just keep the alarm system set, and don't hesitate to call the police at the first sign of trouble."

And what about you? Can I call you?

Casey ran her hand over a small side table and looked at the dust on her fingertips. How did she tell him she was still scared, despite her efforts to be strong? So what that she'd destroyed her old phone and purchased a new one. Some show of strength that was. She was about to voice her thoughts when Jesse strolled to the front door and opened it to straddle the threshold.

On his heels, Casey wondered why he seemed so eager to flee. "Leaving so soon?"

"I have a big day tomorrow, remember? You wouldn't happen to know when your uncle will return, do you?"

So, he was still worried, too. "Funny you should ask. My aunt called this afternoon. She and Uncle John should be home in a few days, meaning I won't have to stay here alone anymore. Then, at some point..."

What? She should get an apartment? Or go back to Oregon?

"At some point, when your troubles with Tannin are resolved, and believe me, Casey, that won't be long—then you'll have to decide if you're going back to your old life in Oregon."

His words stunned her. Hadn't she known that all along? But it was difficult to think past Tannin, to think past her growing feelings for Jesse.

She was considering this when Jesse pressed his lips against hers, and lingered.

He eased away. "The competition begins tomorrow. Be at my studio bright and early."

After he was gone, Casey set the alarm, bolted the doors, and walked through the house one more time, checking all the window locks before getting ready for bed. Climbing under the covers, she held her new TracFone in her hand, wanting to call Meg, but knowing she shouldn't. Not with this new number.

It was going to be a long night.

THIRTEEN

Where are you, Casey?

"You'll be glad when this is over, huh, Jesse?" Miguel asked, pressing the cellophane into place as they wrapped the pieces of Jesse's sculptures.

"You aren't kidding." Jesse blew out a big breath. Miguel didn't even know the half of it. Jesse was working double duty. No—make that triple duty. "I appreciate you helping out on such short notice."

Ricky hadn't come in this morning but called to say he had a stomach virus. Jesse couldn't do this alone and asked Miguel for help. That could work out in his favor. Time spent with Miguel was time spent getting deeper into this operation.

Last night, Eric had informed Jesse that Casey was at the movies with a friend. Good for her. Though she needed to remain alert to her surroundings, the woman could use some downtime or she was going to break.

While she was at the movies, Jesse had stayed at the studio and cut his creations into smaller segments for easier transport. They would need reassembling at the hotel where the competition was to take place.

Earlier this morning, Miguel had come in to help him wrap the pieces into insulated blankets and shrink wrap, though with refrigerated trucks, the measure was mostly precautionary. He didn't want to take any chances where the competition was concerned.

Finishing up the task, Jesse wheeled out the carts they needed to haul the sculptures to the loading dock. "I've got to load my equipment, too."

"You gotta cut ice while you're there?"

"Yeah, it's part of the competition." Jesse lifted the ice—part of a large three-hundred-pound sculpture—onto the cart.

Miguel squeezed his shoulder. "I think you got hired on at the wrong time."

Fortunately, Jesse had his back to Miguel. Did Miguel suspect something? "Why do you say that?"

"It's a lot of extra work. You seem a little stressed, that's all. But you're definitely a better fit than the last guy."

Jesse sucked in a breath. What was Miguel getting at? While they each rolled a cart out of the studio and down the corridor, Jesse grew more concerned over Casey's whereabouts. She should have been at the studio much earlier, but maybe she ended up going to the newspaper first for the morning meetings—except today's activities would be the culmination of all her work on the ice-sculpting article.

That was important to her. She should be here now.

Eric could be trusted to watch her. Jesse attempted to ignore his concerns.

He glanced at his watch, shoving the cart ahead of Miguel.

"You expecting your reporter friend?" Miguel asked.

That Miguel could practically read his mind on most days unnerved Jesse. He detected the teasing in his voice, but he still bristled at the question. "Yes. She should have been here earlier this morning. Once the competition is over, she's done with her story here."

Miguel sighed. "If you say so."

What did that mean?

"I say so," Jesse said, a little harshly, but he couldn't help his rising fear that Casey would end up hurt or, worse, murdered. And Jesse would be the cause. He was in the same position again, having to stand idly by and watch someone get hurt to keep from blowing his cover. If there was any way he could keep that from happening again, he would. He had no way of knowing yet what the cost would be.

Any heinous or capital crime he'd stop if he couldn't alert other agents to stop it in time. But hoped things wouldn't come to that.

He was so close to shutting down this ring and gaining back his reputation in the division. He shoved his cart through the exit and onto the loading dock and held the door open for Miguel.

She could be playing you. Miguel's words came back to him. She could be looking for another story, he'd said. That's exactly what Jesse had suspected in the beginning.

But he couldn't bring himself to believe that about Casey. The woman was too caught up in her own nightmare to give a second thought about what was going on behind the scenes at the ice company.

What Casey didn't know was that Jesse had called in a favor—an agent in Oregon was keeping tabs on Will Tannin.

Nevertheless, Jesse knew he was running out of time.

And right now, so was Casey. He'd stalled for her this morning, but she should have been at the studio an hour ago.

"You ready to roll?" Carlos asked as he hopped onto the ledge next to where the truck was backed up.

Jesse nodded. The guy had lost his snarl since seeing Jesse's handling of the parking-lot stray. Jesse sensed he'd gained a measure of respect from Carlos, but the guy still harbored mistrust. He wondered if Miguel had shared with Carlos the news that Jesse would be making special deliveries.

Miguel helped Jesse lift the wrapped ice-sculpture segments from the cart and into the cold truck and passed them on to Carlos, who stood inside the trailer. Suddenly, Carlos stiffened.

Dread ran up Jesse's spine. He turned to see Casey standing next to the ice sculptures.

When she saw Jesse, she offered a weak smile. "Sorry, I'm late."

"No problem." He took a leap from the back of the truck onto the loading dock platform. He'd warned her about the loading dock. Yet, there she stood. His fault. "But you missed an important part of the process."

Casey scratched her cheek. "Did I?"

She looked from Miguel and Carlos back to Jesse. Jesse would need a chain saw to slice through the thick, cold tension between Carlos and Casey.

He tugged on her arm. "Let's get you into the cab of the truck."

"Uh, no. I thought I'd take my car. That way I can leave when I need to."

Jesse frowned. He'd planned for her to stay with him all day. Eric wouldn't be around that afternoon, having been called away on another assignment.

Jesse was it.

"Well, go ahead then. You can meet me at the hotel," he said.

He needed to get Casey out of there pronto. Did she realize that she was telegraphing all over the place with her continual icy glances at Carlos? Something had happened between the two of them.

What was it?

Miguel reached up and tugged on the trailer door, rolling it down. "Your girlfriend won't be hanging around here much after the competition is over, will she?" Miguel asked, his gaze sliding to Carlos.

Thank you, Miguel. "No, once she's done with this story, she'll be moving to another one she's already working on," Jesse added, just to be sure Carlos caught the information.

Jesse dug in his pocket for the keys—he'd backed the truck up earlier that morning—while trying to ignore how dark Carlos's expression had grown.

"Jesse, the keys are in the truck," Miguel said, squeezing his shoulder.

The guy was trying to help. And here Jesse was, with every intention of destroying the man's life, albeit it a criminal life.

At the hotel, Casey stood inside the roped-off display area where Jesse and Miguel had carted his sculptures along with several blocks of clear ice prepared ahead of time for the competition. The hotel convention center brimmed with sculptors from around the country—and around the world, Casey guessed—eager for a chance to make their sculptures famous.

The room was definitely chilly, but Casey was becoming skilled at dressing for ice sculpting.

Standing back, she took photographs of Jesse at

work, using the camera Danny had loaned her for the day. Should she become officially permanent, she could expense a new one of her own. Or, go back to Oregon and grab the one from her apartment there. The thought brought to mind Jesse's comment last night. *You'll have to decide if you're going back to your old life in Oregon.*

He was right. If the time ever came when Tannin's threats were a thing of the past—no, it was *when,* not *if*—then she'd have to decide what to do with her life. Would she go back to her home in the Pacific Northwest? That seemed the logical answer. But what about the life she was beginning to carve out for herself here? She was becoming accustomed to the climate and beautiful beaches. And what about Jesse and her growing feelings for him?

She focused the lens on Miguel, zooming in, and suddenly, he looked up from smoothing out a section of ice that he and Jesse had pushed together and frowned at her. A hand covered the lens and tugged the camera downward.

Jesse. "What are you—?"

"Miguel doesn't like his picture taken," Jesse said, and shrugged. "It's a weird family thing."

"Whatever *that* means," Casey said under her breath. She pulled up the digital images she'd just taken. Would Jesse make her delete them?

"It means wait until he's gone, or take pictures without him." Though Jesse winked at her, she could hear the strain in his voice, see the tension in his jaw.

She watched in amazement as they assembled the cut segments of the ice sculptures that Jesse had created. Had he really done them himself? Or had Ricky helped? Jesse also assembled a system to pump out the melting water. She might have to see where all that wastewater—if that's what you could call melting ice—ended up. Now that would be the less glamorous part of her story.

"You need me for anything else?" Miguel asked Jesse, but he was looking at Casey.

She wasn't sure she trusted him, but he seemed to like Jesse, she decided, so there had to be something good about him.

"No, Miguel. Thanks for your help." Jesse stuck out his hand and the two shook. Miguel squeezed Jesse's shoulder.

He strolled away, disappearing behind other displays and sculptors preparing for the day. Finally, Casey was alone with Jesse—well, except for a small crowd gathering for the competition. Jesse squeezed her hand, then released it to begin assembling tools on a long table—chain saw, large chisels, drill bits and hand saws.

"Miguel seems like a nice guy," Casey said, "but not so much the other one."

Jesse stiffened. "Yeah, I noticed the tension between you two. You've met him before?"

"You could say that," she said, and lifted her camera to snap a shot of Jesse.

He stopped working completely and frowned at her. "You want to explain?"

"I saw him once before, scratch that, make it twice," she said, then gazed around the neighboring displays, looking for another good angle.

When she swung her gaze back to Jesse he was staring at her.

He swiped the back of his gloved hand over his forehead. "I'm listening."

How could he be sweating in this chill? "That first day I met you—" *when you were acting so strange* "—I ran into him first, only he was on the phone and didn't like that I had interrupted his conversation."

Jesse visibly paled. "How do you know?" he asked, and began stuffing boxes under the table.

Casey could see that he cared about her answer but was trying to look like he didn't. "The dirty look he gave me. Just like he gave me today. And then the second time, he was watching me from the corner of the warehouse as I drove away. Look, Jesse, what's going on?"

Jesse scanned the crowd behind her as he took a step toward her and pecked her on the forehead. "Nothing."

"Then what—"

He tugged her to him and whispered in her ear. "Any more phone calls from Tannin?"

At his reminder, Casey frowned. She shook her head.

"Good. Now, I have to get busy. And so do you."

It was going to be a long, cold day. Jesse tugged on his cap and winked.

That was more like it. When he looked at her like that she felt like all was well with the world. It wasn't, she knew—there was Tannin to think about, but she had Jesse now.

Jesse the sculptor. Jesse…her protector.

She tugged her recorder from her pocket, prepared to talk her way through today's event and transcribe later, though with the noise, maybe that idea wasn't such a good one.

An icicle of doubt threatened her—could Jesse really keep her safe?

His promised protection was all she had, and at least for the moment, it was enough to keep her sane.

Taking a step over the rope that marked off Jesse's work area, Casey strolled across the aisle to snap another photograph of him. He looked adorable in his snug cap, gloves and sweatshirt he seemed to prefer. Amazing he could stay warm while working in his freezer room in only his hoodie.

The downside of today's competition was that her time interviewing Jesse and following him for this article would soon end. Would he still be there for her after that? Casey sighed, hating that her future looked so hazy, impenetrable even—sort of like the white ice Jesse used in some of today's carvings.

How she wished her future were clear.

Someone bumped into her from the side, startling her from her musings. Around her, the crowd had doubled in size and the sculptors were busy, concentrating on their work. Casey had done some research ahead of time and knew the variety of backgrounds represented here, including a few master chefs. She'd like to get an interview with one of the judges, as well. The winner of today's competition would get fifteen thousand dollars cash, five thousand dollars in prizes, and an appearance on a popular culinary television show.

She imagined winning or even being a finalist in this competition could bring her uncle's company more business, but what, besides money, would it bring to Jesse personally?

Validation as an artist? Or did he even care about things like that? There was so much about him she didn't know.

A small sigh escaped. What would it be like to be married to a dreamy artistic type like Jesse? A guy with cold hands but a warm heart, as the saying went.

What in the world was she thinking? Casey groused that her thoughts had traveled to marriage. It was soon, much too soon, especially with her future so unclear.

She didn't even know the guy. Not really. She shoved thoughts of a relationship with Jesse to the back of her mind. She had a job to do. There were so many questions she'd failed to ask because the strain of Will Tannin's interference had hampered her skills as a reporter. She needed to remedy that, and today could be the day.

Enthralled with the artistry surrounding her, Casey strolled down the marked-off aisles and took snapshot after snapshot of sculptors using the tools of the trade. She'd read about an entire restaurant created out of ice. What an incredible medium ice was.

Zooming out with her camera lens, she saw someone...

The face looked eerily familiar, but she lost him behind a towering ice sculpture. Casey lowered the camera and searched the room.

There.

She lifted the camera and zoomed in, finding him again. Alarm shivered down her spine.

There was no doubt where she'd seen him before. He was the guy in the parking lot that night.

His eyes...

She could never forget those eyes, even if she'd only seen their malicious stare for an instant. And they stared at her now.

Casey sagged, dropping the camera to her side. And just when she was beginning to relax, if only a little.

She turned to find her way back to Jesse through the maze of sculptures, not entirely sure which way she had walked, given she'd been completely mesmerized by the artistry. The crowd seemed to thicken around her, and in her rush to be near Jesse, it felt as though people intentionally bumped against her or shoved her back.

Her heart drummed. Her knees seemed to have a mind of their own, growing weaker by the second. Casey's terror was now becoming familiar, the same terror that Tannin had injected her with the last time she'd seen him.

Panic strangled her airway.

FOURTEEN

Jesse pressed the chain saw against the ice, feeling the power in his hands as the machine pulverized the frozen water, spraying powder behind him. He suspected the pluming ice enthralled the crowd the most, especially the kids.

The chain saw carved the ice, slicing into the cold formless block, following Jesse's carefully drawn guidelines for the sleek Pharaoh Hound. He planned for two resting at Ramses's throne, which he'd created at his studio and assembled here.

A small crowd had grown around him, pressing in against the ropes. While he concentrated on the ice, he was keenly aware that Casey wasn't anywhere in his peripheral vision, taking snapshots like she was supposed to be.

Jesse wanted to kick himself for asking her if Tannin had called her again, but her questions about Carlos were absolutely not in anyone's best interest—especially not hers.

Idiot! As soon as she'd entered his life, his handling of this assignment was clunky at best.

Why had he promised her he would protect her?
He wanted to—God knew he wanted to be there for
her. But to make the promise so that she would feel
protected? He took out his ire on the ice and slipped,
missing the line completely, the chain saw slicing
through an entire section of the block.

Gasps rose around him.

The chunk of ice crashed to the floor and broke
into two pieces.

Great. Just...great. He kept a straight face, as if
he'd cut the hunk from the ice on purpose.

Jesse powered down the chain saw and placed it
on the table next to him. He leaned forward on his
knees and caught his breath. He had no idea if his
following recognized his faux pas. The crazy part
was he wondered why he even cared?

He wasn't an ice sculptor. Not really. Yes, he
knew the trade, but he was an undercover agent
who was hung up on a reporter who was in over her
head without even trying. Since he stopped working, the gathering began to disperse if only slightly.

Good riddance.

Think, I need to think. How did he fix this? What
other Egyptian animal or symbol could he make
from the ice?

A bigger problem stared him in the face. How
did he fix the dilemma of Casey being stuck in the

middle of his undercover assignment? Stuck in the middle of his heart?

Was she in the predicament because he'd agreed to the initial interview when all he'd meant to do was keep her safe? What a moron he'd been. Would she be clear of any danger where Carlos or someone in the crime ring was concerned once the competition was done, and her article finished?

All along, Jesse had questioned what Casey had done to generate the sort of attention she was getting. The SUV that had nearly struck her, the man outside the studio—the incidents were unconfirmed as attempts on her life, but forensics took much longer than an hour as portrayed on television. Regardless, Jesse didn't need confirmation to know Casey was in danger. And now, he had his question answered. Carlos thought she'd overheard an important conversation.

Now Jesse had a new question—why was Casey still alive?

To keep her that way she was going to need to cooperate, which meant she shouldn't be wandering far. His gaze traveled through the crowd of families with children, couples, teenagers, gangster types, the works, searching for any sign of Casey. That's when he saw him.

Knife Guy.

Jesse had thought of him as the parking-lot guy until he had pulled that knife on him.

He was dressed differently—no hooded sweatshirt and tough-guy look. Instead he wore nice slacks and a baseball cap, but Jesse would never forget that face. What was he doing here?

Jesse's pulse thrummed in his neck, drowning out all other sounds.

He hopped over the rope and made his way through the crowd. The man disappeared behind a display. Had he seen Jesse and was now trying to hide? Was he here for Casey?

Desperate, Jesse pressed through the throng, looking for Knife Guy, looking for Casey. Someone stumbled into Jesse—or was it the other way around? He couldn't be certain.

He whirled around. "Excuse me."

Then he spotted Knife Guy, standing next to what looked to be a seven-hundred-pound sculpture of Seattle's Space Needle. It rose loftily above the crowd, and it appeared dangerously top heavy.

Jesse gritted his teeth. What had the sculptor been thinking?

Casey stood frozen on the opposite side of the sculpture, staring directly at Jesse. Alarm sprang from her eyes.

Instantly, the hair on his arms and neck stood up.

Screams erupted around him. The icy space needle began swaying. In slow motion, the needle began toppling.

Casey was directly in its path.

A third of a ton of ice could crush her.

"Noooooooo! Casey!"

Jesse flew over the markers, shoved people aside and propelled himself forward, slamming against Casey, pushing her out of harm's way.

The sculpture crashed, sending chunks of ice splaying, and sliding mere inches from where Jesse and Casey lay sprawled on the cold floor.

Jesse covered Casey with his body, protecting her. He hoped he hadn't crushed her himself.

When it was over, Jesse continued to hold her, wishing he could protect her forever.

Casey sucked in air. Her breath had been knocked from her. She groaned, and opening her eyes, saw people gathering around, staring down at her. Some faces frowned, others bore concerned expressions, and still others held open curiosity.

The ache of being thrown to the floor slowly dissipating, she turned her head to the side, only now comprehending that Jesse was speaking to her. That he hovered near like a protective wall.

He peered at her, worry lining his face. "Are you all right?" he asked.

"Sure, but how did you..." Casey pushed herself up on her elbows. "Jesse, did you see him? The man from the parking lot?"

He nodded and climbed to his feet, then offered his hand.

She took it, allowing him to assist her up. "That can't be a coincidence. It just can't be." Trying to hide her trembling, Casey wrapped her arms around herself. Security guards arrived, along with the hotel manager—a suited man in his late thirties—and the event coordinator—a young woman dressed professionally in a dark gray suit.

Everyone seemed to be speaking to Casey at the same time, the questions clouding her thoughts.

"What happened here?"

"Was anyone hurt?"

"Where is the sculptor?"

"Which exhibit was this?"

But their questions accosted her from behind tunnel vision. She squeezed her eyes and rubbed them.

"Ma'am, do you want to file a complaint?"

Casey frowned, unable to respond at the moment. She was still trying to come to grips with what had just happened.

Others answered the questions for her, several explaining that the space needle had fallen over, crashing to the ground. No one said anything about someone pushing it. No one explained that someone had tried to kill her.

Could she simply have imagined seeing the guy from the parking lot lean against the sculpture?

"Can you just give her a minute?" Jesse once again stepped up to the task of shielding her and tugged her away from the chaos into a quiet corner.

Casey was too dazed to consider her responses.

Jesse grabbed her elbow and directed her away from the center of attention, through the growing crowd that pressed into—although security guards were now conducting crowd control—and outside the hotel.

She leaned against him as he guided her, feeling her knees wobble beneath her. "How can you be so strong after what just happened?"

"Because I have to be."

Once at her car, Jesse held out his hand. "Keys?"

"What do you need those for?"

"To unlock your door. You're going home."

Casey was stunned. "But what about my article?"

"You've got what you need, don't you?"

"I…uh…"

"Go home, lock the doors and write your story. You'll be safe at home, don't worry."

"Oh, yeah? What about my uncle's friend and the other intruder who broke in for some reason?"

"The first guy had the code, and the other guy got in because you hadn't armed the system."

Suddenly, Casey's knees gave out, but Jesse caught her against him. He held her tight and stroked her hair. "Maybe I should drive you home."

"No, Jesse. I've done enough to disrupt your day. But aren't you going to tell me I should call the police?"

"Definitely, you should file a report about what happened today. I just don't think it's safe for you to do it here, that's all."

"But did you hear the others? No one said anything about seeing someone push over the sculpture."

"Someone saw it."

"Did you?"

"I saw Knife Guy standing next to the sculpture, that's enough."

"Knife Guy?"

"It's a long story. I'm just surprised no one was hurt."

Casey sighed and eased away from him. "Thank you, Jesse."

"You're welcome." His smile was tender, caring. "I'll call a friend to meet you at your house and check it out for you. I've got something to take care of."

What could *that* be? "You're not going to try to find him, are you?" Now there was a story—that is, on any other day. Exhaustion seemed to infuse her very being.

Jesse didn't respond. Instead he unlocked her car door and opened it for her.

"So that's it. No goodbye kiss?"

He jammed his hands in his front hoodie pocket instead of putting them around her where they should be, then he leaned in to kiss her, gently. It was as if she could feel how much he was holding back. In those few seconds, she sensed how he felt about her. There was so much more than simple attraction, but fear eclipsed anything between them.

A noise disrupted their kiss, and Jesse stiffened then scanned the parking lot. When his gaze returned to her, apprehension replaced any other emotion she'd hoped to see there.

"You did it, Jesse. You saved me today."

"Barely. You shouldn't have left my side. Casey, until I know more about Knife Guy, do not come to the ice company and don't contact me." His stern expression didn't do anything to calm her fears. "I'll call you."

Though she wanted to ask a hundred questions, Casey slid into her car and locked the door then started the engine. Jesse waited and watched as she drove from the parking lot.

Lord, thank You for sending him. Please keep him safe.

Indecision clawed at her. She wasn't sure what to do now. The strong sense that she should run again, find somewhere else to hide, wouldn't let go. But where? And to whom? There wasn't another Jesse Dufour in the world, she was sure of that. With him was the only place she felt safe.

Heading away from the hotel, Casey wished she'd begged Jesse to come with her. Where else in this world could she live and feel safe? It was all too much. Tears slid down her cheeks. What had happened to her resolve to fight back, to fight Will Tannin?

To not let him get the best of her?

Her determination had been nothing more than an attempt to show herself strong, but she couldn't back it up, and any strength she had was quickly crumbling inside. She reached over to dig in her bag for a tissue then realized she'd left something behind.

Danny's camera!

Probably dropped it in the tumble with the ice. She'd have to pay for it, which she couldn't afford. Still, under the circumstances, wouldn't Danny understand? Someone had tried to kill her—she couldn't prove it, but she had her suspicions. And so did Jesse.

Jesse was still at the hotel. He could meet her in the parking lot and help her find the camera. Then she would head home.

She dialed him on her cell and predictably, she got his voice mail. Pulling back into the parking lot, she tried to call him again and left a message that she'd wait in her car for him. No way would she venture back into that crowd with the creepy Knife Guy roaming free.

When she had the opportunity, she'd try to discover if there was a connection between the guy Jesse called Knife Guy and Will, or...Knife Guy and Carlos.

There, she'd given herself permission to consider that possibility.

FIFTEEN

After seeing Casey off, Jesse had made the phone call to McCoffey to report an escalation in the danger she was in and request additional backup. Eric was being pulled from whatever task had taken him from her side today, and was on his way to keep her under surveillance. The news relieved Jesse, allowing him to work on his second sculpture of the day.

Was it his imagination? Or had he drawn the largest crowd yet? He decided people wanted to see a man on fire and right now, Jesse was definitely landing blows on the ice.

He couldn't afford to lose his sham of a job when his mission was so close to its culmination. With Casey safely out of harm's way for the moment, he could focus on the task and then take care of the guilty parties.

Tonight, he'd make sure to pay Carlos a visit and tell him to pull his dog off, that is, after beating the guy to a pulp for his near-fatal threats on Casey. Who else could it be?

Will Tannin was far from Southern California.

He couldn't recall being under this much stress for any assignment—covering the competition to keep his cover, while watching over Casey, while preparing for the takedown of the cash-smuggling ring to happen tomorrow night.

Miguel had passed him the date, time and delivery instructions, which he'd passed to his team for a fully coordinated effort involving several agencies.

Considering the pressure he was under, Jesse feared he was about to fold in on himself, and he worried he'd forgotten the smallest of details.

And that's what got people killed.

By the end of the day, the crowd began to thin out. Jesse accepted that he'd not won, despite the job he'd done in the midst of chaos. When it came time to hang up his hat and move to another department within the agency, maybe he'd consider becoming an ice sculptor instead.

Yeah, right.

He almost smiled at the thought, but it was difficult to allow even the thinnest of grins under the circumstances. Still, he imagined himself in a completely different career, Casey by his side. Now *that* was enough to make him smile. If they could just make it through this, maybe they could have a future together.

That is, if Casey could ever forgive him once she found out the truth of his identity.

Miguel appeared in Jesse's line of vision and stepped over the rope.

"I came back to see if you needed help loading your equipment or what remained of the sculptures."

"Thanks, Miguel. I hadn't thought ahead about clean-up, considering Ricky is sick. He planned that just right, didn't he?"

Miguel lifted his chin. "Too much on your plate."

"You could say that," Jesse said.

He started cording his tools, wishing he didn't have to clean the mess. He needed to find Knife Guy, and...he needed to hear Casey's voice. He imagined her sitting in her living room and putting the final touches on the article, while Eric dutifully kept vigil over the house.

"Say, where's your girlfriend? I figured she'd be stuck to you like glue."

Did Miguel know about what happened? Was he in on the plan? Jesse nearly snarled at him. "I sent her home. I don't suppose you know she was almost killed today. Someone pushed an ice sculpture over."

By the look in Miguel's eyes, Jesse knew the guy had no clue. "Jesse, I'm so sorry. Is she all right?"

Did he really not know what Carlos was capable of? "She won't be all right until I get my hands on Carlos." When Miguel had invited Jesse to be delivery boy, he'd warned him that Casey could be in danger. Jesse thought begging for Miguel's help since Miguel knew he had a thing for Casey would be good enough. "Carlos has it out for her. He's behind the guy in the parking lot and what happened today."

Miguel held up his hand. "Now, hold on…"

"No, you hold on." If Jesse kept talking, he might just talk himself right out of being Miguel's delivery guy. He looked down at the floor, clenching his jaw. At least his reaction was in line with the criminal element, giving no indication he was under cover. "Listen, Miguel, you know I can't stand by and watch her get hurt."

"No one is asking you to. If someone so much as touched my Elena…" Miguel's ire-filled words faded.

Jesse could only imagine the violent thoughts filling his mind.

"Do you need me to help you take her car to her then?" Miguel asked.

The chisel in Jesse's hand slipped to the floor. Blood roared in his ears. "What did you say?"

Miguel stood frozen and unresponsive, his mouth open.

Jesse took a step toward him. "Tell me, Miguel. Where did you see her car?"

"Parked where she left it this morning, right next to the truck."

Jesse hopped over the rope and ran through

the displays now being broken down. He hurried through the exit and into the parking lot.

On the top of the steps from the hotel, he spotted his truck and right next to it Casey's car.

Oh, no...

Casey, what did you do?

Jesse pressed his hand to his forehead and tugged his cell from his pocket. He had two calls from Casey, stating she'd come back to look for her camera. But she planned to wait for him in her car.

What a jerk he was.

He couldn't hear or feel his phone because of using the chain saw. This case would be his last, for more reasons than one.

He dialed her cell and got no answer. The call went to voice mail. "Casey, call me back right now. Where are you?"

He tried again, and then again. Then he called Eric. Man, did he have some words for him.

The guy didn't reply...something had happened. Jesse knew it, felt it deep inside.

A growl escaped. He dialed McCoffey.

A text interrupted him mid-call. Casey's number flashed on the caller ID.

Casey! Thank goodness....

He opened the text to read it.

Did you find the popsicle I left for you? It's your favorite flavor.

* * *

Casey opened her eyes, aware of nothing more than a dull, pounding ache in her head.

What happened?

Where was she? She sat up and surveyed her surroundings, dimly lit by a fluorescent light in the far corner of the room. Her breath came out in big white puffs. She shivered.

Was she…in a freezer?

No…she couldn't be…

But reality slammed her like an arctic blast. Somebody had left her in a freezer. Casey gripped a stainless-steel shelf to steady herself and stood up. Cold stung her fingers.

How long had she been here? Casey spotted the door and, fighting dizziness, made her way to it. She pressed the large L-shaped handle but it wouldn't budge.

Locked. A panic-filled tremor snaked through her body.

How could she be locked in a freezer? Casey shook the handle then began pounding the door. "Help! Somebody help me!"

Then a serious question accosted her. How long did it take for someone to die from hypothermia? Freeze to death? Suffocate?

Casey focused, trying to remember the details of the article she'd once written about hypothermia.

Hikers had been found alive after trying to climb Mt. Hood, but some had died on the mountain.

Of what little she knew, there were three stages of hypothermia. Right now, she was only shivering a little and her hands were numb, but she wasn't confused and could move around.

That's good news.

If she started having trouble moving and was unable to focus, then she should start worrying…

Who was she kidding?

She needed to worry now!

And the bad news? Temperatures in these freezers were below twenty degrees, according to Jesse. She'd spent enough time in the freezer with him to know she'd been here for a while, and without a real coat. All she had was her blazer. She just didn't know how long she had—minutes or hours or days. There were too many variables.

Maybe she could figure out where exactly she was by looking at the contents. Then again, she didn't care where she was, only how she could get out of the freezer.

She sent up a desperate, silent prayer. *Lord, please let it be someplace where Jesse can find me.* And not some random freezer where nobody would guess her whereabouts.

Okay, don't panic.

That Tannin! He wasn't going to get the best of

her. Again, she summoned her resolve, fueling it with anger.

This had to be part of his scheme. He'd told her in no uncertain terms that she would die a slow, painful death. In a sense, knowing that you were going to freeze to death eventually was a painful way to die. At least at the moment she was suffering severe mental anguish. And what made it more painful? Casey wasn't willing to lie down and die.

With chattering teeth, she turned in a circle, looking for what, she didn't know.

Now that she thought about it, her movements were beginning to get sluggish. She rubbed her hands together.

Her gloves? She'd had them in her blazer pocket for the competition. Jamming her hands in her pockets, she searched for them.

Gone. Casey groaned and stuck her hands under her arms. She was a little surprised that she'd been left with her blazer.

She searched the room to get a sense of where she might be and, with any luck, she could find a tool she could use to pry open the door or to communicate with someone on the outside that she was stuck inside. Unless…oh, no…what if Tannin or the parking-lot guy were just outside the door, waiting for her to die?

No. She wouldn't allow herself to think like that. Not if she were going to survive this.

She would focus on getting out alive. She'd focus on seeing Jesse's face again. And somehow, she'd take her life back from Will Tannin. She was done running.

Hadn't God sent Jesse to protect her? God was there for her, she knew in her heart.

Her positive thinking sounded great, but the fact was she was going to die if she didn't think of something quickly.

Pray hard.

Jesse's gut turned stone-cold. If he wanted to save Casey's life, he'd have to keep his wits and not allow fear and anger to cloud his judgment.

He replied to the text.

Where is she? What do you want?

Three seconds without a reply was too long.

There wouldn't be another text.

He didn't have time for this. If he understood the cryptic message, Casey had been left in a freezer somewhere to die. Of course, whoever did the deed was playing with him—either wanted him to find her dead, or wanted to send a warning. With her life on the line, he didn't have time to take chances or to play games.

Miguel came up behind him. Jessed whirled on him and grabbed his collar and shoved his face into

Miguel's. "Where is she, Miguel? What has Carlos done with her?"

The man's face grew red and angry. "Watch who you're talking to, Jesse. I don't know where she is."

Jesse released Miguel and straightened his collar. He believed him, but he wasn't so sure about Carlos. "I just got a text. She's in danger. I think she's in a freezer somewhere."

Miguel looked stricken. "The hotel has freezers. Let's start there."

"Good idea." Without another word Jesse dashed through the door while at the same time he called McCoffey, keeping his distance from Miguel.

Someone had found Eric knocked unconscious near the Helmes' house. Jesse gave McCoffey Casey's new phone number so he could have someone triangulate the location, though Jesse doubted the phone was still in her possession, or that the location could be found in time—jumping through the legal hoops would take at least four hours and as long as twenty-four. That was too long.

Even so, finding the phone or where it was during the call could help them locate whoever was trying to kill her. McCoffey gave Jesse half an hour to find her on his own, after that, back-up would be called in to search for her, which could possibly blow the entire undercover operation.

But a life was at stake.

At the concierge desk, Jesse pounced on the bellhop. "Where's the hotel freezer? Show me."

The guy stood there with his mouth hanging open.

"Now. It's a matter of life and death." Jesse did not want to pull his ICE-agent spiel in front of Miguel, but he would in order to save Casey's life. "The kitchen, show me where the kitchen is."

Looking intimidated, the guy motioned for them to follow. They made their way down a long corridor and soon entered the large commercial kitchen. Jesse didn't bother explaining his reason for being there to the protesting chefs.

"The freezer?"

The bellhop shrugged. "I showed you the kitchen. You'll have to ask one of them."

"I have reason to believe that a woman has been left in your freezer to die!"

Disbelief and shock swept over faces like a wave.

"Over here." Miguel had slipped past the kitchen staff. Without hesitation he opened the freezer and stepped inside, Jesse on his heels. Except for what one would expect to see in a freezer, it was empty.

His spirits plummeted. *Lord, where is she?*

Miguel was right behind him.

"I think we should head back to the ice company," Jesse said. It was the only other logical place he could think of.

"What makes you think she would be there, Jesse?"

The look on Miguel's face told Jesse that he didn't like where this was leading.

"Just a hunch, Miguel. I have no other ideas. You?"

Miguel's shrugged, his expression growing dark.

"I take that back. We can pray."

Miguel almost laughed. "Whatever you say, Jesse, whatever you say. If you think God is going to listen to you, then be my guest."

Jesse felt like Miguel had landed a double-punch in his gut. Miguel had spoken out loud Jesse's deepest fears—with the life he'd lived, regardless of knowing the truth, he'd never been able to reconcile the two. His life didn't reflect his faith—how could it? Working undercover was like living a lie, even though in the end, criminals were hopefully incarcerated and Jesse believed he'd accomplished something good. But could he count on the Almighty to listen to him when he felt like a walking contradiction?

Leaving his equipment and the ice sculptures behind to melt, Jesse climbed into Miguel's truck, allowing him to drive them back to the ice company. Thankfully, Miguel drove as if it was Elena in the freezer.

Jesse regretted even more the lie he'd lived for the past several months. But right now, all he needed to be concerned about was the fact that Casey's life was in his hands alone. While Miguel drove, Jesse dialed the main number at the ice company, hoping someone would answer so he could send them to look in the freezer. But it was after hours, and he got no answer.

"Miguel, what's Carlos's number? If he's there, he can open the freezers and search for Casey."

"Are you kidding me? I thought you said he was responsible?"

"And you think he's not? He threatened her. At the moment, I'm up for trying everything."

"Never fear, my friend, we're almost there."

Miguel raced the truck across the parking lot, flying over a speed bump—which sent their heads to the cab ceiling—and right up to the loading-dock door, locked and sealed for the evening.

He hopped from the truck and jammed his key into the side door, leaving it open for Jesse. "You check the freezer on the far side. I'll get this one."

Jesse gripped the handle of the large refrigerated room where he'd first stumbled on Casey, when she'd gotten lost on the loading dock.

Please, Lord, let her be here...

SIXTEEN

Casey wiped the tears streaming down her face, thankful they weren't icicles yet, thankful for the warmth they brought to her fingers, which grew more numb by the second. She feared she was nearing the second stage of hypothermia.

"Oh, Lord, am I going to die in here?" she asked, her voice barely a croak. But God heard her regardless. He heard her heart's cry for help. She had to believe that.

Thump...

Casey stared at the door for a second before she could comprehend someone was on the other side. She moved to the door and pounded. "Help! Someone help..."

The handle, which she'd been unable to budge earlier because it was securely locked, abruptly turned. Slow to comprehend—relief moved over her like a glacier. The door swung open, and Casey swayed at the sight of Jesse.

"Casey!" He tugged her to him and off her feet, carrying her out of the freezer. "Are you all right?"

Placing her on a nearby counter, he held her head with his hands and peered at her. She could only nod, tears streaming down her face as he pressed her head against his shoulder. He stroked her hair and back, holding her as if he'd never let her go.

"If anything had happened to you..." he whispered against her ear and kissed her hair. "Thank God you're..."

"Alive?" she eased away from him, still chilled.

He rubbed her icy hands. Frown lines creased Jesse's face, making him look much older. "Miguel! Call 911, get an ambulance here."

"Jesse, you could get her to the hospital before an ambulance could get here." Miguel appeared as distressed as Jesse. "The police will want to question her there, too."

"You're right," Jesse said, after a quick glance Miguel's way. He stared into Casey's eyes. "Are you okay to walk to the truck?"

"Jesse, I'm fine. I don't need to go to the E.R." Casey savored that she'd been found; she cherished Jesse's attention.

"You *are* going to the hospital. They'll know how to get your core temperature back up."

She shook her head. "I wasn't in the freezer that long."

Jesse gave her a questioning look, then asked,

"What happened? I saw you drive away. You should have gone directly home." Frowning, he worked his jaw.

The guy was angry. "Didn't you get my message? I waited for you to come out so I could get Danny's camera. Jesse, I would never have done anything so stupid…"

"And yet—"

Miguel nudged Jesse's arm. "Jesse, do we need to have this conversation here? Why don't you take Casey somewhere warm, even if she doesn't want to go to the hospital?"

Jesse scooped her back in his arms. "She's going to the hospital."

As much as Casey loved the feel of his body against hers, of his strong arms carrying her, she freed herself from him, and to her surprise, he allowed her.

"There's nothing wrong with me that a cup of coffee or hot chocolate won't cure. Besides, I don't feel like waiting in the emergency room, and I don't want to be slapped with a big bill."

Jesse frowned. "Are you sure about this? I would never forgive myself…"

"I'm sure. I wrote an article about some hikers who got lost and suffered with hypothermia. I know what I'm talking about."

"One article doesn't mean you're qualified to make the call."

"Please, Jesse…" She watched the desperation in her voice affect Jesse and hated herself for putting the pain in his eyes.

"All right," he said, shoving both hands through his hair. "Let's get you warm, then we can go to the police."

He gave a quick, furtive glance Miguel's way.

"Don't worry about the stuff back at the hotel, Jesse. I'll get some help and get things cleaned up there," Miguel said.

Jesse nodded. Those two seemed to understand each other like brothers. Casey wished she had a friend like that here, wished Meg could be here.

Holding Jesse's hand, Casey allowed him to lead her outside to his Jeep. He opened the door and before she stepped inside, she paused and held his gaze.

"I won't get in unless you promise me you won't take me to the police."

Jesse's jaw worked as he searched her eyes, questions in his. "Why not?"

"Promise me."

"On one condition."

Fatigue setting in, she sighed. "What's that?"

"You tell me everything. Why you don't want to tell the police."

Her momentary exhilaration at being discovered waning, Casey shrugged and climbed into Jesse's Jeep. She was safe for the moment. She was beginning to feel like the only time she would ever be safe was when she was with Jesse.

Except today's fiasco showed her just how vulnerable she was.

Jesse appeared to text someone as he made his way around the vehicle. When Jesse was sitting in the driver's seat and had started his engine, he backed from his parking spot. "If you don't want to go to the hospital or the police, then where?"

Casey rested her head against the headrest, trying to ignore the pain behind her eyes. They had to be beyond puffy right now. "All I want to do right now is get a warm bath, wrap my hands around a hot cup of coffee and curl up with a blanket. Is that too much to ask? Just take me home, Jesse."

Home? Where exactly was home?

"I don't think that's a good idea. Isn't there anywhere else you can stay? What about your friend from the movies the other night? Could you stay with her, at least for tonight?"

"Maybe." Another long breath escaped. "Maybe, yeah, sure. I'd have to get a few things first."

"Okay, then. I'll take you to your uncle's, and I'll keep you safe, while you get a warm bath and grab a change of clothes. But then you need to go somewhere else."

He couldn't know how much his words meant to her. "That's all I want, Jesse. I promise, I'll tell the police everything tomorrow. But tonight, I couldn't stand the thought of sitting there, filling out paperwork, answering questions and then more questions—" her voice broke "—I'm just too—"

"Exhausted." Jesse placed his hand over hers and squeezed. "I understand."

He signaled and turned left onto Shoreline Road and headed to Uncle John's beach house. Glancing at her intermittently, he maneuvered along the curvy road.

"Tell me what happened, Casey. Who put you in that freezer?"

Drawing in a deep breath, she exhaled slowly. "I'm sure it had to be Will Tannin."

"Are you saying you don't know? Didn't you see who it was?"

Tension squeezed Casey's neck. "No, I didn't. I can't remember what happened. One minute I was sitting in my car, waiting on you to call me back." Casey felt heat creep over her, which was a good thing in an odd sort of way. "I know I shouldn't have done this, but finally I got out of the car to go find you. The next thing I know, I woke up in the freezer with a headache."

"Someone probably hit you, knocking you unconscious. All the more reason to take you in." Jesse pulled the Jeep to the side of the road, preparing to turn around.

"I will get out of this car if you don't take me home now."

Jesse glared at her, then his expression softened.

He drove the Jeep back onto the road, heading to Uncle John's.

"Don't you see? I've been through this for months now, Jesse, and I'm so very tired of it. Do you have any idea how crazy I'm going to sound if I say a man has followed me all the way from Oregon and I can't prove it? He's still there. But I think he might have hired the guy who was at the parking lot and also at the sculpture competition."

Jesse didn't respond as he pulled the Jeep into the driveway at Uncle John's.

If she survived this ordeal, she would have to write a story on women who were stalked by ex-husbands. The stats were not on the woman's side. Though Casey hadn't been married to Tannin, he was stalking her nevertheless. Just short of getting the upper hand—of killing him herself—she was running out of ideas.

Lord, help me to get free of this…

Casey wasn't sure she should voice her next thought, but she had nothing to lose. "I'm considering taking things into my own hands. Going on the offense. Will you help me set a trap, Jesse?"

Casey's question nearly bowled Jesse over, and he certainly wasn't prepared to respond. Keeping the lights on the Jeep, he got out and went around to Casey's side, assisting her out.

He rubbed her arms. "Let's get you warm and some food in you, then we'll talk, okay?"

Her slight smile flattened, and she averted her gaze. He recognized her reaction—she thought he believed she was crazy. Pain squeezed his chest. He'd have to set her right.

Once she checked the house and was sure all appeared to be undisturbed, he turned the Jeep lights off. Back in the house, he watched her arm the alarm system.

"Why don't you take that warm bath while I fix us something to eat? What have you got that's good?"

"Help yourself. Pasta's easy and then there are a few frozen dinners."

Jesse nodded and watched her make her way down the lighted corridor to the guest bath and bedroom.

Once she was out of sight he pursed his lips and made a fist, wanting with all that was in him to plunge it through the wall. Any normal man would have called an ambulance and the police. But Jesse wasn't normal. He was a guy with a mission.

The police would have secured the loading dock to investigate the crime scene, and that was the only reason Jesse had allowed Casey to have her way.

That, plus, Jesse knew something she didn't—he knew who had been threatening her and why. It wasn't her Oregon stalker. Carlos had it out for her and had left her in the freezer. But tomorrow night, it would all be over. Carlos would go down with the crime ring. Everything hinged on that, and tonight's incident threatened to blow it all.

Months of work could have been blown!

Jesse wanted to wring Carlos's scrawny neck, but maybe Miguel would do that for him. Putting Casey in the freezer at the ice company was beyond stupid and could cost them everything if the police got involved.

But…Carlos wasn't that stupid. The man had left Casey in the freezer as a warning to both her and Jesse. That had to be it. That's why Carlos had texted Jesse to let him know where Casey was. He wanted him to find her before it was too late. Still it was a huge risk on his part. Casey could have died, or she could have insisted on reporting the incident to the police. Even Jesse had come very close to getting backup from his fellow ICE agents in order to save her. He'd texted for them to stand down once he found her.

Not wanting to stay here one minute longer than necessary, Jesse busied himself with making Casey something to eat. That would warm her and give her energy, and maybe she could think more clearly.

What Jesse didn't know was how much longer he could keep Casey in the dark.

She wanted to set a trap? Could he keep her out of trouble just one more day?

He was walking a shaky precipice between keeping her safe and doing his job—one wrong step and they could both die. She meant far more to him than this job, but if he could keep her safe and out of harm's way for only a little longer...

Jesse liked to think his many skills included whipping up a mean dish of pasta. But tonight, as he accidentally dumped the entire container of garlic salt into the sauce, he knew his mind was not on the task.

He found another can of tomato paste and started all over. He was glad Casey agreed to stay at her friend's house and hoped her friend would agree to have her. Of course, then they ran the risk of involving yet another person in Casey's drama.

Jesse grabbed the cup of hot cocoa he'd made. He strolled down the corridor to find Casey. Standing next to the closed door, he didn't want to disturb her privacy, but he needed to know she was all right and deliver the warm drink.

He gave a light rap with his knuckles. "How are you doing in there? The pasta's almost ready."

The door whipped open. Dressed in a lavender sweater and blue jeans, Casey smiled up at him, looking more beautiful than he'd ever seen, but with a distant wariness in her eyes.

His mind went blank. Why had he knocked on her door?

"Oh, is that for me?" she asked, and took the mug of hot chocolate from him.

"Yeah." He stared down into her eyes. At that moment, the events of the day seemed to crash down on him, almost crushing his heart. He cared far too much for this woman. Almost losing her today brought his long-ignored feelings to the forefront.

"Come here," he said. Mindful of the hot chocolate, he pulled her into his arms and pressed his lips against hers.

A tiny groan escaped her throat as she melted into him.

Oh, Casey, I think I love you...

A noise from the kitchen startled him, and he ended the kiss. "Uh, I think the pasta is boiling over."

Leaving her behind, he hurried back to the kitchen. After pouring the water off and mixing the sauce in, Jesse fixed Casey a bowl and found her sitting snug on the sofa, wrapped in a blanket.

"Here you go. I hope you're hungry."

"Mmm. It smells wonderful."

Jesse joined her, sitting across from her on the other sofa. They ate in silence for a few minutes, his mind filled with everything he wanted and needed to say. He hadn't a clue where to begin. He assumed Casey was equally preoccupied.

She finally set her bowl on the coffee table. He frowned when he noticed how little she'd eaten and set his bowl down, too.

Casey rested her head against the sofa back. "This is a very strange ending to a very strange day, don't you think, Jesse?"

He hated that she was going through this. "Are

you feeling warm enough now? Care for a walk on the beach?"

"Are you serious? With that madman out to get me? What am I going to do, Jesse? Maybe you're right. Maybe I should have gone to the police. This was an actual attempt on my life."

That was all it took. He had to tell her the truth.

He left the spot where he sat and slid onto the sofa next to her. Casey's eyes widened but he saw pleasure in their depths, making him want to kiss her again. Making him want to lay his heart on the table.

But…he didn't know how. Was he even ready to admit how he felt about her to himself?

And he knew, without a doubt, that what he was about to share with her would change everything. McCoffey had made it clear to tell her nothing about this operation, especially in light of her career choice, but he had to find a way to keep her out of harm's way.

Yeah, right. This freezer incident was the absolute last straw. Jesse saw that now.

But…looking into her eyes, he saw, too, that revealing his true identity now could crush whatever they had between them—it would destroy her trust in him.

Relationships were built on trust and he knew, had always known, that he could never have a relationship while working undercover, living in this role he played.

He slid his hand down her arm. "There's something I need to tell you."

In her eyes he saw confusion and hurt and even a flicker of—could it be hope?

"Jesse, what is it?"

Maybe he could take his time telling her the truth, and in those moments he could enjoy what he had with Casey, even in the face of adversity. A walk on the beach could go a long way to calm her frazzled nerves and make it easier for her to hear what he had to say. He hoped.

"Walk with me." Jesse stood and held his hand out to her.

Casey's expression was troubled. "Let me grab a jacket."

When she returned with a jean jacket, looking gorgeous, he wished he'd taken her somewhere nice. He wished tonight's conversation held a completely different backdrop and tone, rather than Casey's being in danger. Not wanting a repeat of the last time they'd gone for a walk on the beach, he made sure the alarm was set, then they strolled onto the deck.

Jesse had to tell her everything.

Except, he wasn't sure he should tell her how deep his feelings were for her, or that he had any.

Focus, man.

Keeping her safe, keeping her alive, was more important than his feelings. If they both made it out of this alive then they might have time to explore a future together.

SEVENTEEN

Casey loved the feel of Jesse's hands, his fingers intertwined with hers as he led her down the steps and onto the beach, but it seemed surreal. "I had two attempts on my life today, Jesse. Somehow I feel like a walk on the beach is crazy." She was here only because Jesse had something to tell her.

A salty breeze enveloped her and somehow calmed her. There was maybe half an hour of sunlight left—they could watch the sunset together. But the timing was wrong, all wrong.

"I brought you out here because you're stressed." He stopped walking and turned her to face him, the breeze lifting her hair and blowing it from her face.

"Of course I'm stressed. I have no idea how to escape Will Tannin." The tears pressed against the back of her eyes again. She drew in a breath to stop them. "I want to be strong and fight this, but I don't know how. Now you're telling me to relax."

"Honestly, I hope the guy shows up, because I

promise you, when I get my hands on him you'll never have to worry about him again."

Casey took a step back. "Well, he was there today and you weren't. Don't you see, Jesse, you can't protect me. Not really. This is all so crazy."

And what was more crazy? She loved Jesse. She longed to be in his arms. She longed to tell him how she felt about him. If only...if only Tannin—

Jesse took a step forward and grabbed her arms. "Casey, that wasn't Will Tannin's doing."

"What? What are you saying?" How did Jesse know anything about it? "You don't believe me, either?"

Now *that* hurt. Of all people, she thought Jesse believed her.

"This was someone else."

"I don't understand. What are you talking about?"

"Let's walk some more."

Casey obliged, strolling next to Jesse, but growing more impatient by the second. "Just tell me what you know about Tannin."

"I'm not who you think I am," he said, continuing his walk.

The air grew too thick to breathe, and Casey's legs seemed to carry her on automatic. "Who are you?" she asked, her voice sounding like she was in a tunnel. Hadn't she ignored the little niggling about Jesse Dufour—the niggling that something was amiss because she couldn't find anything about him? The little niggling when he acted so strange at the ice company?

She was in love with a man who wasn't who he said he was.

Dizziness swept over her. She dropped to the ground and sat in the sand, feeling a heavy weight against her chest.

Jesse plopped next to her. He took her hand. She yanked it free, pain slicing her heart. "Just tell me who you are."

"I'm an undercover agent, working to bust a crime ring at the ice company."

Casey lay down, feeling the soft sand against her back. She squeezed her eyes, letting the tears slip down her temples. "That explains a lot. Why you didn't want me on the loading dock that day. Why didn't you just tell me?"

"Don't you understand? I'm not supposed to tell you now. But you're in the middle of it. I don't want to see you get hurt, nor do I want you to keep worrying about Will Tannin. He's still in Oregon. I'll deal with him, but one thing at a time."

"Then why didn't you just tell me to go away? Shouldn't I just disappear now? Get out of town? Can't your agency protect me?"

Jesse heaved a long, hard sigh. Looking up at the few stars beginning to appear, she could see from her peripheral vision his hand against his forehead.

"That would seem like the logical choice, but it's far more complicated than that. In order to keep you safe, I'm supposed to keep an eye on you—keep you from snooping around for a story because you're a reporter—this coming from one of the men in the crime ring. Somehow that hasn't gone right, but I have every intention of correcting it. Then there's the matter that you're not even supposed to know what I'm telling you now."

Casey rolled onto her side, propping herself up on her elbow to look at Jesse, love flooding her heart. "And how can they watch me if I'm not even supposed to know about the operation? Is that it?"

"Actually, there has been someone watching you to protect you, someone other than me." He glanced over at her with an impish grin, then it turned apologetic. "I'm sorry they failed. But if you leave town, there is Tannin to consider. What if he finds you again?"

"Can't your people keep protecting me?"

Jesse shook his head. "Not officially. It's not what we do. That's a matter for the police. That's why I think it's best if you stay with your friend for a few nights, just until this whole thing blows over."

"You think I'll be safe there?"

"I think that's the best place for you right now. There will be someone keeping watch over you, but Casey, promise me you won't say a word about any of this. If you do, you could blow everything I've spent months working for. If you do, you could get us both killed. Do you understand?"

"I think so, yes." The cool earth seeping into her

bones, Casey got on her knees to stand. Jesse beat her to it.

"You must be getting cold out here. I'm sorry, I just wanted to be free of the house for this conversation."

Jesse helped Casey to her feet. Now that she knew the truth about him, everything made sense. And somehow, knowing that Tannin wasn't after her at the moment eased her mind. Jesse would take care of everything else.

He was a good guy, just as she'd reassured herself in the beginning.

"You really are a hero," she said.

Casey searched his eyes, and what she saw took her breath away. Just like she wanted and longed for, he tugged her into his arms again and kissed her.

Thoroughly.

Warmth flooded her, chipping away at any remaining chill she felt from the freezer, deep down to the marrow of her soul. Waves caressing the beach sounded miles away. She wanted to tell him what was on her mind, in her heart.

I love you.

Not yet. She needed to hear him say the words first, if he even cared for her that much.

"Oh, Casey," Jesse murmured. "I was so afraid I would lose you with the truth." He deepened the kiss.

But wait...

Casey untangled herself from Jesse, startling herself with the abrupt move. Jesse looked torn. Stunned.

"Why did you say you wanted to talk about this away from my uncle's house?"

Jesse looked a little dazed and frowned.

"It's been all about my uncle's house from the beginning, hasn't it? The intruder wasn't necessarily after me, was he? What does my uncle—"

"Casey, Casey—" Jesse held out his hands "—you're getting way ahead of yourself. Just let me answer."

"I'm listening."

"Yes, we believe your uncle could be involved. It's part of my job to determine the players."

Casey closed her eyes, thinking of Jesse and Miguel. "And Miguel?"

"Look, Casey, the less you know, the better."

"And Miguel?" she asked, louder now.

When she opened her eyes, Jesse was staring at her. His silent answer was enough. A vice squeezed her lungs. Miguel and Jesse were close; she'd seen it with her own eyes.

"You are using me to get into my uncle's house, to get close to him when he returns. You act like you care when you don't. It's all about your job, isn't it, Jesse?"

"That's not—"

"You're using me, just like you've used Miguel."

Anger and hurt wrapped around her heart at the same time. Casey turned her back to Jesse, wanting to get as far away from him as possible.

Casey ran away from Jesse, taking his heart with her.

Taking his hopes…

God in heaven, I need Your help!

She headed down the beach and in the direction of the house. He sprinted after her, knowing that he would catch her.

And then what?

How could he have made such a mess of things? How could he make her understand?

Casey glanced behind her and when she saw him, she ran even faster. Should he chase her? Or let her go?

But she was in danger. He had to make sure she didn't do something crazy.

Breathing hard, Jesse caught up and reached for her. She stumbled and fell forward.

Jesse caught her, saving her from a nasty fall, and whirled her to face him, careful he didn't hurt her. "Please, you have to believe me, no matter what things look like to you, I…"

Her eyes flooded with tears, and she fought to free herself from him, but he held on. He had to make her understand. No matter what else happened.

"Casey, I love you. Can't you see that?"

For a fleeting moment, Jesse saw hope flash in her eyes before the pain set in.

"Tell me the truth. That night you happened down the beach and saved me from the man checking on the house. Why were you there? Spying on the house? Spying on me?" Questions spewed from her in hot, quick breaths.

"That was never my intention. My only concern for you was and still is your safety."

"You haven't answered my question."

Jesse glanced around. They were near the house now, near the neighbors. The light from the Helmses' deck showered them now. "If you don't mind, can you turn the volume down a little? People can hear."

"Well?" she asked, a little softer, heaving with anger and mistrust.

And hurt...

Oh, man...

He'd blown things with her in a big way. There was no going back.

"Yes, I was watching the house, but when I heard you scream, I had already gone back to my jog. Will you just trust me?"

"You mean like Miguel trusts you? I saw the bond he has with you, Jesse. Does he know who you really are?"

"Look, I don't like this any more than you do. The operation will be over soon, if you can just stick with me a little longer."

"How could you?" Her face contorted with a tsunami of tears. "How could you endear yourself to me like that? Making me feel..."

Jesse's throat tightened at the possibilities hidden in her words. He took a step toward her, his face near hers.

"What, Casey?" He searched her eyes. "What do I make you feel?"

"Nothing." Her gaze focused on something behind him. "I feel nothing for you."

He didn't believe her. But it didn't matter. Something cold and hard wrapped around Jesse's heart. He was all business now, like he should have been from the beginning.

"Casey, this isn't about feelings, it's about your life and mine. It's about busting a ring of criminals who committed a murder, among other crimes." Jesse could hardly stand to look at her, knowing he sounded cold and professional. He shoved a hand through his hair.

She took a step back and folded her arms, but said nothing.

"I'll help you pack what you need and escort you to your friend's home. There will be someone watching over you. Maybe you can even call in sick for a few days until this is over."

She sniffled. "I don't believe you about my uncle, you know? I'm going to prove you wrong."

"You just don't get it, do you? Lives mean nothing when millions of dollars are at stake. You go nosing around, and you'll get both of us killed."

EIGHTEEN

Inside the beach house, Jesse paced the living room and waited for Casey to pack. Fuming at Casey, fuming at himself, he tried to ignore the gaping hole in his heart.

If he looked too hard, he'd see that he was bleeding all over the place. Funny how his desperate need to keep anyone from getting hurt during his undercover assignment ended up hurting that person in an entirely different way.

And he was hurting, too. Casey had been a distraction from the beginning, and it could cost them both. He swiped a hand down his face. Somehow he had to shrug off the crazy way she made his heart pound, his crazy need to be with her, to kiss her and hold her.

Somehow he had to move past all of that in order to adequately protect her. In order to finish his assignment successfully and come away unscathed.

Yeah, right.

After all these years of playing a part when working undercover, he should have enough practice at keeping his emotions in check. He should be able to harden his heart—and he was at the freezing point until Casey walked into his life, and unfortunately, smack into the middle of a cash-smuggling crime ring.

Why, God?

Would he get an answer? Probably not.

Did he deserve one? No.

He tugged back the long, heavy drapes that covered the expansive window, and peered out. His nerves were stretched taut, given the threats on Casey's life today.

Everything would go down tomorrow night, and he still had more than his share of work to be prepared for the takedown. He massaged the back of his neck, growing more impatient by the minute. He should never have kept her here so long. Then again, he doubted there would be another attempt on her life tonight.

What was taking her so long to pack?

His cell rang. *McCoffey.*

"Yeah," Jesse answered, regretting his venomous tone.

"Finally found where the call came from."

"Great." Four hours later.

"Helms Ice."

"Figures."

"And the tire had evidence of tampering."

Well, that was record time. Did it even matter

anymore? He already knew someone wanted her dead. A dull ache started in Jesse's temple. "Is that it?"

"No, it's not. Just one more night, Jesse. Are you going to be able to hold it together that long? Or am I going to have to pull you from this case, too?"

"I've got it," Jesse said, gritting his teeth. What did the man think? All his previous failures rushed through his mind in a flash—a man beaten within an inch of his life while Jesse watched, drug dealers suspecting he wasn't one of them. All of that getting him pulled from an assignment before he got himself killed. The pressure slamming against his temples.

Everything came down to tomorrow night—every detail had to play out exactly as planned.

"One more thing. We think someone else is running the money, not Helms himself."

"Interesting." Jesse glanced around the room to make sure Casey wasn't in earshot.

"Where are you now?"

"I'm in the house."

"Can you—"

Jesse heard a noise and whirled around to see Casey glaring at him, a satchel over her shoulder and luggage at her side.

"No, I can't." Jesse hung up. He'd given them the thumb drive he'd found; there wasn't anything else lying around in plain sight.

Casey rushed by him to the garage door. He drew in a breath, wanting to explain.

"I don't even want to hear it," she said, and opened the door to the garage, where she obviously expected to see her car.

"What are you doing? My Jeep is in the drive."

Casey stopped, but kept her back to him.

"Your car is still at the hotel," he said.

She sagged against the door. "I was going to take it over to Tessa's. There's no need for you to drive me. I'm a big girl."

"Look, Casey, I'm sorry about everything. I know you don't believe me…" But now wasn't the time. "I need to make sure you're safe. Let me at least see you to your friend's house. Promise me you won't do anything stupid."

"Take me to my car, Jesse. It will seem strange if you drop me off there. I've already called Tessa, and she said I could stay. Besides, I need my car to go to work in the morning."

Casey's tone was aloof, calloused. But Jesse could hear the strain. It was costing her.

Just one more night and the sting operation would be over. Just one more night and he wouldn't have to worry about keeping Casey safe from Carlos.

"All right, Casey. You win." To his deepest regret, she could be out of his life forever. But maybe that was for the best.

Casey slid into her car after Jesse looked it over, both inside and out. It crossed her mind to start the engine, leave the parking lot and just keep driving.

She could drive right down Main Street and keep going, eventually hitting the freeway. But she was beyond tired and had no place to go except back to Oregon.

Jesse sat in his Jeep, and through his windshield, she could see him staring at her. She knew he was waiting for her to leave the parking lot so he could follow her to Tessa's house where some unseen agent would supposedly watch over her.

She'd seen how that worked.

Oh, Jesse...

She did as he expected, knowing there was nothing else she could do. Pulling onto the street, she accelerated and watched in her rearview mirror the Jeep's headlights as Jesse tailed her. Hopefully, that was all she would see. She'd had enough drama to last a lifetime.

Following the directions Tessa had given her, Casey finally arrived at 2127 Lone Palm Drive. She encouraged her little green car into the driveway and parked behind Tessa's Honda Civic. No matter, they could leave at the same time in the morning.

Casey climbed out and glanced around. She'd lost Jesse's tail at some point, but he probably wanted to be invisible like the other agent.

Her throat constricted. Had she actually stumbled into a sting operation? Man, if her life weren't on the line, what she wouldn't give to get that story. To think her instincts had told her something was up from the start. She'd effectively ignored them.

Yanking her satchel, purse and luggage from the car, she slammed the door and made her way to the small front porch.

Tessa stood in the doorway, smiling. "What took you so long?"

"Jesse dropped me off to get my car. I forgot I left it at the hotel."

"Hmm, that sounds interesting." She grabbed Casey's luggage as Casey followed her into the house.

"Don't even go there. It's not like that." A pang shot through her heart. "I was there for the sculpture competition, remember?"

"That's too bad," Tessa said. "I thought you two had something going."

Casey sighed, too tired to explain.

"I'll show you the extra bedroom and then you can tell me why you needed a place to stay."

Stepping into the small but neat little room, Casey skimmed the contents. A country quilt on a queen-size mattress. She remembered how comfortable the bed was at her aunt's house and doubted Tessa would have expended that much money on a mattress. Still, she was grateful to be here.

Tessa set her luggage on the bed and Casey followed her lead, laying the rest of her things on the mattress, as well. "I can't thank you enough for letting me stay on such short notice."

"No problem. I could use the company. Had a

blind date tonight. It didn't work out, at least for me. Get unpacked, and I'll make some popcorn."

Casey slumped onto the bed. She so didn't want to eat popcorn and stay up all night with girl talk. How safe was she at Tessa's home, anyway? Had she brought harm to her coworker and friend by coming here?

"Tessa, you've got an alarm system, right?"

The woman paused in the door and studied Casey. "Things are that bad, huh?"

Behind her eyes, Casey detected a smile, and she grinned. "Yep."

"Well, let's go make sure it's set. I only remember to arm the thing half the time. I grew up in a very small town. We left the keys in our cars, never locked the doors, that sort of thing."

Casey followed her down the hallway and into the kitchen, where Tessa set her alarm by the back door.

She glanced at Casey and stuck popcorn into the microwave. "There, feel better?"

Sliding into a kitchen chair, Casey laid her forehead against her arms on the table. "What have I gotten you into?"

Tessa laughed. "I should be the one asking you what you've gotten me into, shouldn't I?"

The aroma of popcorn permeated the kitchen. Casey couldn't think how to answer.

"I can tell you're about to crash. Forget the popcorn. Just go to bed."

Casey rose. "I can't thank you enough for your help."

"Oh, you will, girl, you will. I want to know all about your mystery man."

In response, Casey offered a weak smile and nodded as she plodded out of the kitchen. In the guest room, she readied for bed. She didn't think she could sleep but she had to try. She had every intention of finishing the ice sculpture and competition article for Danny tomorrow. Though she might not be a lot of things, she was a professional. After she explained everything that had happened, he had to understand and pay her for the article, although—to her chagrin—he might simply put the money toward the camera she'd lost.

Even if he did pay her, it wouldn't be much, but maybe enough to allow her to skip town for a couple of nights until it was all over. Until Aunt Leann was back in town and then what? She wasn't sure.

Maybe Tannin's threat would have died a silent death by then, as well. Casey slid between the sheets, relishing the comfort of a warm bed. Though she didn't know Tessa that well, her actions were that of a friend.

Casey closed her eyes, but her mind was spinning with the events of the day. Twice, she almost died. Twice Jesse saved her.

Jesse...

He had told her he loved her. She'd dreamed and hoped he would feel that way about her. And there it was, but the circumstances in which he'd confessed his love didn't work for her.

Had it been Jesse the agent or Jesse the man who loved her, that had saved her today?

She rolled over to face the other wall. How could she know if Jesse loved her or not? She couldn't believe a man who worked undercover, especially considering all the time he spent with her, pretending to be someone else. And he had an ulterior motive for wanting to be close to her.

Some investigative reporter she'd turned out to be. Although, to be honest, she had resolved not to probe when her reporter senses picked up on the strange vibes at the ice company. She'd been true to that resolution—but now she was paying for it. She'd told Jesse that she was going to investigate to prove her uncle's innocence, but she'd been angry and hurt.

If her uncle was involved, Casey would do what she could to find out the truth—but only after Jesse's mission was complete. She couldn't have his blood on her hands.

Or hers, for that matter.

Everything was set.

Jesse had given the other players—his superiors

and team members—the information about the time and place of the money drop and they, along with local agencies, would be ready to rain down on the ice-and-trucking company.

Tonight was the night that arrests would be made.

All on Jesse's signal. His chest ached with the weight of it.

As Jesse paced the parking lot near his Jeep at the ice company, he tried once again to get through to Casey. Forget her cell, he called information and got the newspaper's number.

"Orange Crossings Times," a smooth voice answered.

Jesse was momentarily impressed to hear an actual person, rather than a computerized message center, take his call. "Casey Wilkes…er…Carson Williams, please."

"May I tell her who is calling?"

He cringed. Giving his name might reduce the chances she'd answer. "Jesse Dufour."

"One moment, please."

As Jesse paced, waiting for Casey to respond, he spotted Carlos driving through the parking lot in his little red truck, heading back to the loading dock. He hadn't seen the man since yesterday. Pure rage shot through Jesse and, still pacing, he squeezed his free fist.

He took several long breaths, knowing he couldn't let his anger blow things for tonight.

"I'm sorry, sir, she's in a meeting. Can I take a message?"

"Yes." Jesse seethed and relayed for Casey to return his call. He had no doubt that she was avoiding him.

Casey, please don't go forward with your threat to prove your uncle's innocence. Just stay away tonight.

He marched around the side of the building, preparing to face off with Carlos.

Warning sirens wailed in his head. He squeezed his fists and relaxed them repeatedly until he finally made the entrance. No truck was backed up to the loading dock, waiting. Instead the large opening yawned like a dark cave.

Footsteps resounded from somewhere in the shadows, then Miguel came into the light. "Jesse! My man." He held his hand out to assist Jesse up the ledge. Jesse ignored his hand and hopped up without Miguel's help.

He pressed past Miguel. "I'm looking for Carlos."

Miguel grabbed his shoulder. "Leave it, Jesse."

"I don't think so."

Carlos stepped from behind a large box, legs spread wide and hands on his hips. "Did I hear you say you were looking for me?"

Though Jesse still saw respect in Carlos's eyes, he also saw agitation. Jesse moved into Carlos's space, pressing his face inches from Carlos and grabbing his shirt in his fists. "You stay away from Casey, do you hear me?"

The man's face turned red with his scowl. Jesse prepared to receive blows. Instead, Carlos threw his hands up, holding them out flat.

Jesse tensed at Carlos's unexpected reaction. "Do you hear me?"

Miguel stood at Jesse's back. "Let him go, Jesse."

"He could have killed Casey." Jesse considered he could blow the mission if he pressed further, except his actions were how the game was played. He, too, knew they wouldn't get another delivery boy just because he confronted Carlos.

He had to be tough. They would know something was off if he wasn't.

Carlos pressed his hands against the wall, showing his unwillingness to engage. His non-action sucked the steam from Jesse's train and he eased up, but only slightly.

"I swear I didn't touch her. Miguel told me you were with her."

Miguel squeezed Jesse's shoulder, the familiar action coaxing Jesse to ease off. "You're our brother now, Jesse. Carlos might not like your girlfriend, but I assured him, because of you, she wasn't a threat."

Jesse struggled to breathe. "Then…who?"

Miguel shrugged. "I found this."

A knife? Jesse immediately recognized it. "The guy in the parking lot. He's not working for you?"

Laughter exploded from Carlos. "You think I

would stick that dog on your girlfriend? You think I would stir up trouble for us here so the police would come again?"

He had a point.

"I don't know who he is, Jesse," Carlos said.

Jesse looked at Miguel and saw confirmation. Miguel had stuck by Jesse, trusting him, making sure Casey was safe, at least from any harm Carlos could do. Acid burned Jesse's gut.

Tonight, Miguel would find out Jesse's true identity. He swiped a hand down his face. If it wasn't Carlos who had tried to harm her...

"Casey..." he said, her name a whisper on his lips. "I've got to go."

Jesse jogged away from his new brothers and hopped from the loading-dock ledge. Once inside his Jeep, he sped out of the parking lot and headed to the newspaper. He called his contact in Oregon.

The call went to voice mail. "Jon, I need to know Will Tannin's status." And he needed to know who the man was talking to, but that required warrants, and this situation was completely out of their jurisdiction. McCoffey would have a fit if he knew Jesse had been working this.

NINETEEN

Casey sat at the desk in her cubicle at the *Orange Crossings Times* and allowed her head to roll forward. She pressed her palms against her forehead and pulled at her hair, feeling the tension in her scalp.

What was I thinking?

When she'd come in this morning after tossing and turning all night, she'd looked forward to the distraction of completing this article for the newspaper. Her plans were to finish, proving she was the consummate professional even in the face of complicated circumstances.

Complicated wasn't the right word. It didn't come close to describing what she was going through now.

Pathetic. She was a journalist unable to think of the right word.

She stared at the story on the computer's screen. Images of yesterday's trauma scorched through her mind. Heaviness pressed against her, weighting her head and neck, the emotional and mental damage a struggle to bear.

Releasing a deep sigh, she knew, too, that she needed to speak with Danny about the camera. Right now, she had no images to go with yesterday's competition, or rather she had no images that she had taken.

Plenty had flooded into the local news station with her picture via cell phones and other digital media—images of the fallen sculpture with the headline Frozen Space Needle Almost Kills.

She didn't even want to consider that if someone had caught everything on video it could be available on the internet.

Her image could be all over the television. Jesse had convinced her that Knife Guy, as he called him, was connected to the crime ring and that the loading-dock man thought Casey had overheard an important conversation and now he wanted her to die from an accident.

Then why stick her in a freezer and lock the door? Could that look like an accident? Things weren't tracking but her brain was so muddled at the moment, she couldn't sort things through.

One thing she knew to be true. If Tannin hadn't found where she was hiding before the ice-sculpture debacle, he would now.

Maybe she should have kept driving last night. Why hadn't she?

Danny had scolded her for coming in today, and he didn't even know the half of her troubles. Still, the sooner she completed this story, the sooner—

"At least there's some good news," Danny said from behind, startling her.

Already on edge, she jumped in the chair and whirled it around to face him. He dangled the camera by the strap. "We have the camera back," he said.

Casey couldn't decide whether to be ecstatic at the discovery or disheartened that she would have to look at the images now—all reminders of yesterday, all reminders of Jesse.

She reached for the camera and forced a smile. "Yeah, I don't have to buy you a new camera."

His head came up. "Did you think I would make you pay after what happened? I didn't want you to come in, remember? You're not looking too good. Why don't you go home? Just send me your notes, and I'll finish the article."

"I'm already here, so I might as well finish." Besides, being here, surrounded by people, was probably safer than being somewhere alone. "Mind if I ask how you got the camera back?"

Danny pointed at the case where it said, Property of Orange Crossings Times in capital letters. "A hotel employee found it, I think. Someone was kind enough to drop it off."

Casey looked at it with suspicion. "What are the chances?"

He tilted his head. "I'm sorry?"

The chances that someone would be that honest. "Nothing."

"Are you sure you don't want the day off, at least? I'll leave the article until you're ready if that makes you feel better."

If she were a reporter worth her weight, she would be excited about all the stories she could write from this incident. Right now, she felt like she'd been reduced to rubble, and she was thankful for Danny's sensitivity. When she'd first asked him for a job, he'd contacted Eddie, her editor in Portland, who explained her predicament. Danny wanted an exclusive on her story—the real story—but after things had died down, just as they discussed from the beginning. The *Orange Crossings Times* had a story online about the Space Needle sculpture toppling, but the focus was on the sculpture and the crowd, and thankfully, not on Casey.

Casey shook her head. "Nope. I want to finish. But I do have a request."

"What's that?"

"If I finish this to your satisfaction, can you pay me for it today?"

"Sure." The editor studied her, concern edging his face. "I'll take care of that for you."

Casey sagged with relief and nodded, offering a thin smile. Danny hadn't pressed her, but seemed to understand her needs, even when she didn't.

He nodded and left the cubicle. She turned back to her computer screen.

Danny Garcia, you're one of the good guys.

But then, she'd thought Jesse was a good guy. Her cell buzzed on the desk.

Jesse...

She'd ignored his repeated calls today.

Casey, I love you. Can't you see that? No matter how hard she tried, she couldn't free herself from the haunting words. Oh, how she'd wanted to hear them.

But...not like this.

How could she know if Jesse's words were true? A man working undercover who'd befriended others in the process in order to gain intelligence could not be trusted.

At least not with her heart.

Casey pushed away from the desk and stood. She turned and came face-to-face with Jesse.

At the sight of him, she sucked in a breath as her heart began to pound. Her head swam with his cologne.

"What are you doing here?" she asked. It was all she could manage to say.

Jesse didn't respond. Instead he stared her down, myriad emotions playing in his eyes. Casey held her breath, reading fear, anger, hurt and...

Love?

No, she couldn't go there. She averted her gaze. "Jesse, I..."

"Come on." He grabbed her elbow, his touch making her knees weak. Yet she stiffened, not wanting to expose herself to any more pain.

He ushered her from the cubicle. Casey tried to resist, but it was impossible unless she wanted to make a scene in front of the newspaper's few employees. At the moment, Jesse's presence had drawn only a modicum of attention. Still, though she allowed him to escort her from the building, she made sure he knew she wasn't happy with his surprise appearance.

Jesse's grip on her elbow remained even as they exited through the front door. As soon as they were out of earshot next to the side of the building, Casey yanked her arm from his grasp.

"What do you think you're doing?" she asked with as much vehemence as she could muster. She teetered on the edge of crumbling.

"Why didn't you answer my calls?" he asked, matching her tone.

"I'm working."

"On the ice-sculpture story? Don't you think you need to answer my calls?" He lowered his voice when a man and woman walking past glanced at him. His face was near hers now.

"I have all I need about the story, thank you," she said, and made to leave. "Now, if you'll excuse me."

"Not so fast." He grabbed her arm again. His words reminded her of the first time they'd met when he'd stopped her from leaving the office.

She glared down at his hand, and he slowly released it.

"What more is there to say?" she asked.

In response, Jesse stepped into the shadows of the building's corner and jammed his hands into his pockets.

Reluctantly, she joined him. "I'm listening."

Man, he wished he'd met her another time. Her lush hair was pulled back in a clasp behind her head, but a lone strand hung down her face. He wanted to touch it, feel its smooth silkiness—just like her face. She'd tried to conceal the circles under her eyes with makeup.

He'd done some of this to her, he knew, but not all of it.

"You're only working on the ice-sculpture story, right?"

Casey glared at him. "Since when do I have to tell you the stories I'm working on? It's none of your business."

Wow, he couldn't have dreamed her viciousness would stem from his confession of his career choice last night. Unless, of course, she cared. And from that, he drew hope.

"Since you told me that you were going to prove your uncle's innocence, that's when. Casey, promise me you'll stay out of it. I can't guarantee your safety unless they think I've got you under my thumb."

"I don't believe you can guarantee a thing. Everything that happened to me yesterday was while I was supposedly being guarded by one of your dogs, remember?"

She had him by the throat. His ears were ringing as if she was choking him.

"What's the matter? Nothing to say to that?"

I got nothing.

Jesse wished he knew exactly what was going on—who the Knife Guy was or was working for. He wasn't prepared to tell her that her Tannin was possibly behind things, after all, not until he was sure himself. Nor could he share that he didn't think Carlos and Miguel were behind the attempts on her life because she might relax, or believe she was safe to investigate and prove her uncle's innocence.

Everything was just…convoluted.

Saying nothing more was best for the moment. She would be safe at her friend's house and safe at the newspaper, as long as she stuck to the sculpture story. Sharing anything new could disturb the precarious situation further. Right now she was a fragile sparrow. He feared she'd flutter away out of his reach and into harm's way.

But there was one thing he needed to convey. "Look, we believe your uncle is innocent, okay? There's no need for you to prove anything. Just stay away from the ice company. Don't even come there to talk to me about the story."

Her shoulders sagged. He took a risk and placed his hand against her cheek, cupping it. To his surprise and pleasure, she closed her eyes. He savored the emotional charge her reaction sent through him. He savored this moment with her—it could be his last.

Oh, how he wanted to tell her, to convince her how he really felt.

Casey, I love you...

She opened her eyes and stepped back, as though only then realizing she'd dropped the wall she'd raised. Her momentary lapse was gone. "Is that all you have to say to me? I need to get back to work."

"That's all."

Casey looked down at the sidewalk. "There isn't anything else you want to tell me?"

What did she want to hear? Yes. He loved her. But she wouldn't believe him, just like she didn't believe him last night. Besides, the next time he told her that he loved her—if he got the chance—would be under different circumstances. Better circumstances. "Right now, your safety is the most important thing."

"My safety or your job?"

Jesse frowned. Couldn't he have it both ways?

"Sorry. I shouldn't have said that. I want you to be safe, too, Jesse. Don't worry about me. I'll be all right." She stared at him, her eyes searching. Her soft lips hung open, and he sensed there was more she wanted to say.

Shaking her head, she turned from him. He let her walk back into the building.

Jesse allowed his gaze to roam the street, seeking out the hidden agent who watched her.

There, just across the way. In an instant, their eyes connected and just as quickly, Jesse moved on.

Casey rushed through the door, putting distance between her and Jesse, though with all her heart, she wanted things to be different between them. She headed to the ladies' room and pushed past a woman leaving. Once inside, she leaned on the counter to catch her breath.

Slowly she lifted her head to peer at herself in the mirror, noting her pallid complexion and the shadows under her eyes, despite her attempt at concealment.

Should she have told him she decided to leave? How would he have reacted? At this point, why did she care? It wasn't like she could trust a word he said.

Casey hated herself for being so hard on him. He was just doing his job, wasn't he? And if he succeeded, criminals would be caught—murderers and smugglers would be arrested. The person who'd left her in the freezer to die would be arrested, too. And if Jesse didn't succeed?

Would he come out alive tonight?

A sob caught in her throat. *God, please, protect him....*

The restroom door swooshed open, and Tessa stepped in.

Her face brightened then slipped into a frown. "You okay?"

Tensing, Casey stood tall and examined her reflection, brushing the hair from her face. "Sure. I didn't get much sleep last night."

Tessa washed her hands, though she hadn't used the facilities. "You sure you don't want to talk about what's going on?"

"It'll all…" *be over tonight.* Casey caught herself before she said too much.

In his studio, Jesse intermittently paced the room while shuffling papers around on his desk. It had already grown dark outside. He glanced at his watch. Eight-thirty.

He checked the tiny mic in his collar again and tugged his baseball cap containing the small camera to fit snugly on his head. He slid his hands around his belt to his back where the holster was secured and kept his SIG hidden.

Though pat downs and weapons searches were part of the risk, he'd dug himself deep enough that he was beyond that requirement. He hoped. Still, they couldn't expect him to make deliveries like this without protection, could they?

The SIG would remain hidden until the moment of truth.

At ten, he would head over to the loading dock. Miguel had asked Jesse to be the delivery man, but tonight he would assist them in receiving the cash, too—the plan, to stack it between slabs of dry ice that had already been prepared.

Brilliant.

The refrigerated truck making the delivery would also carry ice cream and other frozen perishables. Jesse would drive to the border, where another driver would take the truck through.

But Jesse was here to witness that transaction and keep things from getting that far.

Adrenaline pumped through his veins. He'd worked for months to find and expose the matrix of participants in the cash-smuggling ring, and still he'd not gotten much past Miguel and Carlos and now possibly Spear. Once these men were arrested, they'd need someone willing to provide more detailed information about all the players.

And finally, now, the operation had come to the point of a takedown. Tonight, he would be a witness to the money drop. Tonight, ICE agents would catch the perpetrators in the act, which always resulted in a much stronger case than arrests for crimes already committed.

And tonight…Miguel would discover the truth about Jesse.

Jesse squeezed his eyes shut and calmed his racing heart. He couldn't allow his heart to bleed for the man who'd called him brother. Miguel knew exactly what he was doing in committing this crime.

Miguel, why did you do it, man?

Jesse leaned against the counter and gripped the edges.

Even now, local agencies were preparing to pounce

on the ice company when Jesse signaled the drop had taken place. Agents were getting into position at both the company and the airport to keep anyone from fleeing the scene or worse, the country.

With all the information that Jesse had gained, an attorney had already gotten the search warrant signed within the last couple of hours, and all that was left was to initiate the takedown.

It all came down to Jesse…and perfect timing.

And then Jesse would have proven himself to his fellow agents and to his superiors. He could request a transfer or quit entirely, but all with a good reputation and clean conscience.

Well, maybe not a clean conscience, but he would have to work on that. And maybe they wouldn't forget his failures, but at least he would have redeemed himself in their eyes.

His cell rang. Casey?

He snatched it up, chiding himself that he couldn't get her off his mind. His heart hammered at the sight of the caller ID.

Jon, his contact in Portland.

"Jesse. I've lost Will Tannin."

The door to Jesse's office swung open. Miguel leaned in and, noticing Jesse was on a call, waited.

"Gotta go." Jesse ended the call, knowing he needed more information. "What's up?"

"What are you doing? We need you."

"I thought you didn't need me until later."

"The guy's here early."

Perfect timing, yeah, right. Jesse walked next to Miguel down the long corridor, feeling like someone had taken a sledgehammer to his plans.

"If you do good, Jesse, there's more work for you."

Jesse wanted to tell Miguel he wouldn't let him down. A brother would cover his back.

Miguel opened the exit onto the loading dock, and before Jesse could pass him, he grabbed his shoulder. "You don't want to mess this up."

Jesse nodded, feeling the gravity of Miguel's words. Now they were getting to the crux of the matter.

No, Jesse didn't want to mess up. For his sake, or for Casey's. And for the first time, he realized what it was about her that he needed, that drew him to her. She gave him something to live for. She gave him a future worth living for.

Casey...

He wished he could call Eric and give him the heads-up about Will Tannin. But he was in the middle of the final act in this scene. As soon as he finished this, he'd find her and keep her safe.

Forever.

Oh, Lord, give me the chance to do that.

Jesse walked a little behind Miguel, following him. A truck was backed up against the loading dock and a man stepped around Carlos and stared at Jesse. Hard.

Spear!

TWENTY

Casey finished packing the few remaining items and zipped up the suitcase.

"You're sure about this?" Holding a cup of steaming coffee, Tessa leaned against the doorframe of the bedroom.

"I'm sure." Casey gave a halfhearted grin and lifted her satchel and bag. Then she laid them back on the bed. "Listen, Tessa, I'm so grateful to you for letting me crash here."

"You're more than welcome." Tessa set the coffee mug on the small writing desk and stepped toward Casey. "I was hoping you'd tell me what's going on, but since you haven't said a peep..."

Casey shook her head and lifted a hand to stop Tessa.

"Let me say what I have to say. If you're in some kind of trouble I want to help." Tessa's eyes teared up, and she blinked, looking away from Casey. "I came to Orange Crossings to escape an abusive situation myself, so I can give you an understanding ear."

"I'm so sorry…"

Tessa swiped her eyes. "I've never told anyone about this."

Casey hugged Tessa then released her. "I'm glad you found a safe place, but don't worry, my situation isn't like that at all."

She considered her words, wondering at their accuracy.

"Okay, as long as you're being honest with me. And even if you aren't, I want to help if I can."

Casey felt bad that she couldn't share more, but the less Tessa knew, the better—at least about Jesse's covert operation at the ice company. Jesse had assured Casey that Tannin wasn't the immediate threat, but with her picture possibly in the news and on the internet, Casey believed now more than ever that she had to leave—if only for a few days.

Once Jesse was free from his current undercover obligation…

She drew in a breath. In that case, she might seek his help. After all, he'd been the only one to offer protection.

Could she ever shake free from her outrage that he'd used her?

With one last hug, Casey said her goodbyes to Tessa and climbed into her little green car. She was on the road again to only the Lord knew where. With a quick glance in both directions of the street, Casey backed the car out and shifted into first. If there was an agent watching over her now, he was definitely invisible.

Casey headed toward Main Street. From there she'd take Shoreline Road back to her aunt's house for a quick stop to gather the rest of her things. She wouldn't even go back if it weren't for her stupid diary. But she had to get the diary.

If Tannin somehow got his hands on that—

She shuddered, not wanting to think about what he could do with the information. Plus, she really would have no place to hide if things continued on this course. Anyone she'd ever known was in that diary.

She'd stayed late at the newspaper to complete the ice story, proving herself the professional she was. To her credit, Danny had seemed pleased. How strange it was to write a story such as that, when she was right in the center of a far more intriguing story. As soon as this was over, Danny would have his exclusive from her.

If it weren't for her need to fall back into obscurity, she'd be there, waiting as soon as those men were arrested. How she'd love to smirk at the one who tried to silence her—that Carlos.

Driving down Main Street, Casey could see the ice company in the distance.

What was going on there at that very moment? Was Jesse arresting the bad guys, or had the deed already happened?

Regardless, she hoped no one spotted her little

green car and misunderstood, thinking she was up to trouble. But surely no one would notice her from this far away.

She turned left on Shoreline Road and sped up. In her rearview mirror, she spotted lights emanating from the loading-dock side of the building—not so unusual. The men worked late at times, depending upon delivery needs.

But she saw no flashing lights that would indicate the police were there.

Lord, please, please keep Jesse safe.

Her hands trembled against the steering wheel. Finally, she arrived at the beach house and zipped into the driveway. A few lights remained on as she'd left them, and the house looked as it should. She didn't bother to drive into the garage—she wouldn't be that long. Knowing that someone was watching out for her reassured her. Still, she wanted to be smart.

Get in and get out...

That was quickly becoming her mantra.

If the alarm was tripped, she'd know something was wrong. Casey eased the front door open and glanced at the alarm. It blinked, which meant it was waiting for her to enter the code.

Alert to her surroundings, Casey flipped on lights as she trotted down the hallway, making frequent glances behind her. What an idiot she was. If she was this paranoid, why had she even come?

Relax. Tannin is in Oregon. The bad guys were with Jesse tonight. And Casey had protection.

In the guest bedroom, she opened the closet and sighed with relief, like she expected someone was behind the door.

Her big suitcase sat in the corner, undisturbed. Casey yanked it up and flung it on the bed. She opened it and began pulling the rest of her limited wardrobe from hangers and tossing the items into the luggage. The action reminded her of when she'd first fled Oregon. She hadn't considered that she would be staying away from her aunt's house for an extended period when packing to stay with Tessa. She could have taken it all then.

As things stood, she couldn't be certain if she would return.

And that stupid diary—where had she put it? She searched the nightstands and under the pillows.

Her heart nearly broke at the thought of leaving Jesse behind for good. Never knowing for sure if the words he'd spoken were true. Now she understood what he meant when he'd said that all that mattered right now was her safety. She felt the same way about him.

In the end, the most important thing was his safety, and she continued to pray for that. She zipped the luggage and skimmed the contents of the room. Her aunt had mentioned returning in a few days, though she hadn't given Casey a specific date.

Casey wanted to leave the room like she'd found it. Spotless.

But she didn't have time to fluff the pillows. She had an increasing sense of unease and blew out a breath. She needed to leave now.

Where is that diary? She bent to look under the bed. There.

Her diary was under the bed along with…? What was that? The *Lladro* figurine. With everything that had happened, Casey had completely forgotten about it.

On her knees, she slid her arm forward, reaching for the diary first.

Pop, pop…

Casey pulled back from under the bed, bumping her head and leaving the diary.

Gunfire!

Pop, pop…

Glass shattered somewhere in the house.

Casey froze, her heart seemed to stop, then pounded erratically.

No!

Not again. This couldn't be happening again.

Glancing around the room, she searched for a weapon and spotted another figurine. That tactic didn't work so well for her the last time. Her cell was lying around somewhere. Or was it in the car because she'd been in a hurry?

The landline phone was next to the bed. She lifted the receiver to call 911. No dial tone.

Hands shaking, she almost shrieked.

This was for real.

No case of mistaken identity. At that moment, Casey knew she had one option—to get out of the house. To escape through the bedroom window was the only way out. She ran around the bed to the window where darkness stared back.

Pain seared her scalp as something—or someone—caught her hair, snapping her head back and bringing tears to her eyes. She screamed and squeezed her eyes. When she opened them, she was staring into the eyes of a madman.

"Tannin!"

"You thought I wouldn't find you," he said, his sour breath hot in her face. "I've known where you were all along."

Hands still gripping her hair, he crushed her face down into the carpet as though to smother her. Then he yanked her head up again enough for her to breathe and for him to press his face near hers, making sure she had to look into his eyes. See the death wish there.

"Will, no, please…" Her voice sounded like someone else's, trembling, begging.

"You had no idea who you were messing with when you started that article!" He was yelling now.

Casey felt the last of her will to fight trampled under the terror he was raining down on her. "No, you're right. I didn't have a clue. I'm so sorry."

"And you still don't know." He tightened his grip

on her hair. "It doesn't matter, because sorry isn't good enough. It's too late for me and now it's too late for you."

Oh, Lord, please help me!

"What are you going to do?"

She asked, knowing she was going to die. There could be no doubt. If there was a time for Jesse to save her, now was it. But she knew where he was—he was fighting his own battle. She couldn't wait for him.

Tannin grabbed her wrists and flipped her over, venom in his eyes. He reached for her throat. Casey begged him with her eyes and searched the room for something—anything—that could help her. But as the pressure closed around her throat, choking off her air, she knew it was hopeless. She groped for the bed post with one hand and the dresser drawer with the other. If she could pull a drawer out...

It was impossible.

Speckles of light began edging her vision. Wait. The figurine was still under the bed.

Could she reach it? She stretched while fighting unconsciousness.

Gripping it with her hand, it felt solid and heavy. With all her strength—*please, Lord*—she slid it from under the bed and swung at Tannin's head, slamming it into his temple.

His eyes rolled back and he loosened his grip, releasing her. He fell over next to her. Hands at her throat, Casey gasped for breath and climbed to her feet.

What had happened to the agent who was supposed to be watching her? Was that what the gunfire was about? Was he injured or dead?

Tannin groaned. Casey wasn't going to wait around for him to rouse. Unfortunately, he was between her and the door. Dare she step over him? What if he woke up and grabbed her?

She made for the window, her original plan, and opened it then slipped through and landed on the deck. She ran around the house and climbed into the VW.

Slipping her fingers into her pocket, she freed the keys and started the ignition. Casey peeled from the driveway and watched her cell slide from the passenger seat into the space between the seat and the door.

The only way to reach it was to stop the car and climb over the seat or get out and walk around. Forget that.

She would drive directly to the police station— they'd believe her this time about a crazy man trying to kill her. The guy had been in her aunt's house. There would have to be evidence all over the place, including her neck. If only Tannin would follow her directly there, then she could get her life back.

But things never worked out so easily.

A quarter of a mile up the road, bright headlights filled her rearview mirror, nearly blinding her.

The vehicle was big, had to be a truck or SUV, and judging by the aggressive approach, she knew it was Tannin.

He slammed into the rear of her car. Casey's head whipped back against the seat, sending pain through her neck and shoulders, and reigniting the throb in her head.

Ignoring the pain, she pressed the gas pedal to the floor.

Come on, come on, come on!

Climbing the hill, the VW couldn't accelerate enough. Soon, they'd approach the bend in the road.

The vehicle behind her bumped her again. To her horror, the driver pulled right next to her on the left.

He was in the wrong lane.

Headlights appeared up the road, heading directly toward them. Casey glanced over. She couldn't see inside the SUV. Was he going to back off, or what?

She'd better slow up herself, unless she wanted to be part of this collision.

Before she released the accelerator, Tannin slammed into her from the side.

Her car veered off the road and went into a spin.

Casey steered into the spin, trying to maintain control.

She'd been knocked too far to easily get back on the road, and then the car skidded to a stop. The airbags deployed. Stunned, Casey sat still, trying to comprehend it all.

She knew she had to get back on the road. Taking in her surroundings, realization dawned.

Déjà vu. This was the same place where she'd gotten the flat and been forced from the road. Was that the same SUV that tried to run into her before?

She searched the darkness and spotted the vehicle up the road.

Upside down.

And what happened to the other car? Surely if they hadn't been involved in the wreck, they'd call the police.

Casey attempted to disentangle herself from the airbags. Could she even start her car now? Even so, how could she steer the thing with this mass of nylon fabric hanging all over? Casey freed herself and clambered from the car.

Breathless, she glanced up the road again.

Was Tannin...? Had he survived that? Could she leave him? She jogged up the road and approached the flipped vehicle. She leaned over to peer at the driver's side. If Tannin had survived, what then?

Buckled in his seat belt—he'd had time to do that?—Tannin hung upside down in his seat. Blood oozed from the side of his head and dripped down to what under normal circumstances would be the ceiling of the cab.

Tannin began to stir. The seat belt had saved his

life. If Casey's car had flipped, she was certain she wouldn't have been so lucky, because she hadn't buckled.

In the distance, Casey saw the lights from the ice company still shining bright. Despite the danger there, the lights were a warm invitation. With Tannin stirring now and her car inoperable, what choice did she have?

She recalled the several times Jesse had been there for her. And even if he couldn't help her tonight, even if he was caught up in the sting operation, she could at least hide somewhere because she still had the key to his studio.

And maybe, just maybe, the madman chasing her would be the one to stumble into Carlos at the wrong time.

The hairs on the back of Jesse's neck stood erect as he sliced blocks of dry ice into ten-pound slabs, wearing protective gloves. The cash would go between the slabs. He thought when Miguel had told him the guy had arrived early, he was speaking of the man delivering the cash, but no, it was Harrison Spear.

Jesse had already had one run-in with him at Casey's house. He'd been the one to drop the incriminating thumb drive.

Jesse had no doubt he wanted his property back. When Jesse stepped from the back of the truck onto the concrete of the loading dock, Spear was talking to Miguel. He eyed Jesse with distrust.

Was he about to lose control here? Lose his life, too? Though he'd wanted to prove himself one last time, if he had things to do over again, he might choose to quit and go away with Casey, make a new life together.

But now he might have completely blown it with her and lost that chance, as well.

He made his way to Miguel, ignoring Spear's looks, trying to act like he was clueless to the man's personal issues. Approaching Miguel, he said, "What next?"

"Don't be impatient, Jesse. We're waiting for the delivery."

"But the sublimation time is counting down."

The sound of a vehicle entering the parking lot sent a mixture of relief and tension through Jesse. Since Spear's arrival, his apprehension had climbed a few notches. If he could get Miguel alone, maybe he could find out what the guy was doing here—or maybe this was all part of the process. It seemed logical to ask to be introduced, but then, he'd already met the guy at the Helms's house, and he wasn't sure bringing that up in front of Miguel or Carlos at the moment was for the best.

Besides, Spear himself didn't appear eager to disclose that they knew each other. He, too, had something to hide.

Jesse barely caught the smirk before it crept over his face.

There was no reason to smirk. Spear suspected something. Jesse could feel it in his bones. The vehicle, which Jesse now saw was an old silver Buick Roadmaster, pulled next to the refrigerated truck. That made sense—it had a sizable trunk.

He held on to his cool veneer, but his pulse thrummed through his veins.

This should be the cash.

The driver—a man Jesse had never met—popped the trunk to reveal a case about four square feet. Jesse would guess the case held, depending on the size of the bills, anywhere from half a mill to a mill and a half.

His throat constricted.

Carlos and Spear pulled the case from the trunk of the car and slid it onto the edge, where Miguel and Jesse lifted it into the back of the truck. They both climbed in and worked quickly to stack the cash between the slabs. Though the truck was well ventilated, Jesse wasn't of a mind to die from asphyxiation tonight. He had a job to complete, and hopefully, a woman to love.

Suddenly, Carlos jumped into the back of the truck.

"Someone's here," he said with a scowl and pulled a gun.

Had one of the agents reacted too soon? Jesse hadn't given the signal yet.

"Who is it?" Miguel asked.

Jesse wasn't in a good position to signal for back-up, but he might have no choice.

"Jesse's girlfriend. It was like I thought, Miguel. She can't be trusted." Carlos lifted his chin, defiant. "And neither can he."

Oh, no! He couldn't signal them now, not with her here. She could get killed.

Miguel looked from Jesse to Carlos and pressed the gun Carlos held toward the floor. "I'll check it out," Miguel said.

"I'm coming, too," Jesse said, his blood raging to the boiling point.

What are you doing, Casey?

Carlos stared Jesse down as he passed. "Miguel! We do not have time for this."

"So get to work," Miguel said. Spear leaped into the truck, apparently eager to get the cash stashed into hiding.

"Come on, Jesse," Miguel motioned for him to follow.

Furious, Jesse thought he would explode.

I don't believe this!

Had she fooled them all? Jesse squeezed his hands into fists and followed Miguel.

He needed to signal to the others, but in doing so, Casey could get caught in the crossfire. He had to assess this new threat first. Again, timing was everything.

And what would he do if they actually found her?

Jesse wished he could pull his gun, but that might tip his hand too soon. They exited the loading dock next to the truck and jogged around the side of building where Casey had been seen.

As they neared the corner, Miguel peeked around, Jesse right behind him. "Look, Miguel. Let me handle Casey."

Miguel lifted a finger to his lips then slid back from view. "There's someone after her."

"What? What makes you say that?"

"I saw a man jump from the shadows. He looked roughened up, bloody, even from this distance."

"Was it Knife Guy?"

Miguel shook his head. "I don't think so, never saw him before. He went in the side door to your studio."

Jesse and his brilliant idea to give Casey a key.

Miguel moved to slip around the corner, and Jesse tugged him back. "Let me take care of this, okay? She's my problem."

For the first time, Jesse thought he saw doubt in Miguel's eyes, but the man only nodded. "We're brothers, Jesse. I trust you."

Miguel crept back toward the light from the loading dock. Jesse tried to numb his mind against Miguel's words, knowing what Miguel would soon discover about him. The sour taste of bile rose in his throat and he spat it out.

Whoever was after Casey—if it was related to the crime ring or if it was the infamous Will Tannin who had apparently skipped town—Casey was running for her life.

Of that, Jesse had no doubt. Otherwise she would never have come here tonight, knowing the danger she was in. Knowing the danger she would put them both in by showing her face.

He crept around the building to his studio and slipped inside, gun at the ready. He made a quick search and discovered it empty, then slowly moved through the maze of corridors in search of Casey.

He had to keep his anger in check. He reminded himself that she knew what was going down tonight and the only reason she would be here was because she thought that was her only choice.

Because Jesse was here. She'd told him that he really was her hero; that, after he told her about his job—well, at least before she decided she couldn't trust him *because* of his job.

Casey was nearly out of breath, but she couldn't give up now, not when she was close to surviving this maniac's attempt to kill her. She'd run as hard and fast as she could away from the scene and turned in time to see Tannin climb from the SUV and make his way toward her.

Aware that he was following her, she led him to the ice company, knowing she could use that to her advantage. She'd avoided running directly into the gaping entry of the loading dock because she saw the men there, Jesse among them, so she'd used the key Jesse had given her.

If she could somehow draw Tannin into the warehouse and loading dock, make him the target. But how?

Lord, I have no idea what I'm doing here, but I see no other way. Show me the way. Protect me!

Quietly, Casey sneaked around cold storage bins and the machines used to make both block ice and dry ice. A hand clamped over her mouth.

Her scream was stifled. The memory of the first time Tannin had done this gripped her. What would come next?

From behind, he pressed his mouth against her ear. "Now I'm going to finish what I started. How appropriate that you should die here. I'll put you in the freezer when I'm done. This time you won't escape."

Casey kicked and struggled, but to no avail. Why had God made men so much stronger? Tears burst from the corners of her eyes. Before she could gasp for breath, Tannin had her pinned on the ground and put his hands around her throat.

Not again!

His hands ripped away from her throat. Casey opened her eyes.

Jesse!

He held Tannin by his neck. "What do you think you're doing?"

Casey coughed and choked, trying to gasp out the words, "Jesse, it's Will Tannin."

Jesse scowled. "That's right. I hardly recognized you from your internet picture. You've got blood all over your face."

TWENTY-ONE

Jesse had longed for the chance to have a go at Tannin. But the timing was all wrong. He needed to be on the loading dock, witnessing the transaction. He should be signaling for the team to make their arrests.

His rage and frustration at the circumstances were meriting, but he held himself in check. Will Tannin rammed his head into Jesse's gut, slamming him into a wall. Together, they fell sideways.

Tannin knocked over a container. A block of dry ice clunked onto the concrete as Tannin stumbled and fell into the fog. His scream yanked Jesse from his storm. Jesse could only imagine Tannin's pain. At -109.3°F, his skin at the contact point would die, leaving a burn blister or worse, frostbite. Plus, the gas would asphyxiate the man if he didn't get out of the fog.

Jesse yanked Tannin from the brink of further bodily damage, then reached behind and snatched his gun, swinging it around to aim at Tannin.

Tannin stared at his hands, pain etching across his face, then looked at Jesse. "Go ahead. You might as well kill me."

"I'm not going to kill you," Jesse said. The coppery taste of blood filled his mouth. "But you're going away for a long time."

"For what?"

Standing in the corner, Casey's breath came in torrents, her face a mixture of terror and anger. "For stalking me, that's what. For trying to kill me, that's what."

A strange laugh escaped Tannin as he slowly blinked and glanced at Casey. "The police have yet to prove anything. I see no reason to stop."

"Well, they will now. I'm an ICE agent, and you'd better believe that I'm wired."

Now that he'd contained the situation, and unfortunately, given out his identity, he needed to give the signal.

"The ice is hot!" The authorities would immediately descend on the ice company. Jesse needed to get Casey to safety. But Tannin blocked her path.

"On the ground," Jesse said, directing his command at Tannin. "Now!"

Jesse had to work fast. As Tannin appeared to drop to his knees, Jesse held one hand out to Casey, motioning her from behind the captive.

Instead of falling to the floor, Tannin rushed Jesse, catching him in the knees. He plummeted backward, banging against the concrete.

His gun slid away from him.

Despite his burns, Tannin wrapped his hands around Jesse's neck.

In the background, he could hear gunfire. Obviously Carlos and Miguel weren't going to surrender without a fight.

Tannin was a big man and also well-trained. No matter what defensive tactic Jesse used, he couldn't budge the guy from his throat. His head was about to explode.

He needed air.

Miguel's face loomed behind Tannin, then suddenly, Tannin stumbled off. Jesse sucked in a deep breath. He rolled to his knees and scrambled to his feet.

Where's my gun?

Ahead of him, Tannin grabbed the SIG. Jesse didn't wait for him to use it, but yanked Casey behind a stack of giant crates. Miguel appeared around the other side of the crate, empty-handed.

He shrugged, seeming to understand Jesse's silent question. "Carlos is the one who packs, not me."

Jesse nodded, pressing against the boxes and shielding Casey. "How much did you hear?" he asked, keeping his voice to a whisper.

"Enough." Miguel's hard expression was tempered with the pain of betrayal.

His reaction startled Jesse, but he didn't have time to process what it meant. "Why did you help me?"

"Because the Cordovas never turn their back on

family, no matter what. Besides, your fight with Casey's stalker has nothing to do with you and me. He's a bad man."

Grasping at Miguel's words, Jesse released a sigh. Sweat beaded, dripping down his temples and his back. Miguel backed away from Jesse and Casey, slipping around the corner of the boxes and into the shadows.

Miguel had saved his life. And that, after hearing what Jesse told Will. But why? Had Jesse misjudged Miguel all along? Could Miguel have served as an insider? An informant?

Jesse blew out a breath, realizing he should have worked the situation differently, and now, he should follow and arrest Miguel. But the sound of gunfire kept him planted next to the crates with Casey. Without his own gun, he was useless.

All he could do was pray, and for the first time in what seemed like a lifetime, he felt at peace doing just that. Like God would listen. The only reason he knew that now was because of Miguel's actions. The man was loyal. If a man betrayed can be loyal, how much more can God?

I will never leave nor forsake you...

The words gripped his heart, and Jesse knew beyond a doubt that God had been listening, but Jesse hadn't wanted to talk.

"Where's Tannin?" Casey's breath was soft against his neck. He had her pinned between him and the box, protecting her as best he could.

Carlos, Spear and the other driver were likely attempting to hold off the agents, at least for the moment.

He shook his head then pressed his mouth to her ear. "I need to get you somewhere safe and out of the line of fire," he whispered.

Dread consumed her eyes. She squeezed his arm. "No, Jesse, stay with me."

He slid his hands to cup her face, his fingers slipping through her mass of hair. "I won't leave you, I promise, until I know you're safe."

"I'll never be safe as long as Tannin is free."

Or alive...

"I don't want you to get hurt or killed," she said, her whisper barely audible.

Jesse searched her eyes, knowing that now wasn't the time—but he couldn't help himself. She'd thought he'd been using her. Had she forgiven him? In her eyes, he saw everything he needed to see. She loved him.

But would it be enough?

The gunfire subsided. Voices and footsteps resounded in the warehouse. Jesse sagged against the box.

It was over.

Suddenly, Tannin stepped into the aisle between the crates, aiming Jesse's gun at them. The man's hands shook, making Jesse nervous. Even if he didn't intend to shoot, he could do so accidentally.

"Freeze!" The shout came from somewhere outside Jesse's line of sight. "Lower your weapon."

Tannin made to follow the instructions.

But just as he'd pretended to obey with Jesse, he went through the motions with the agent behind him until the last possible second. Then he turned and fired the gun. In return, he received answering gunshots, his body rocking back and forth.

Casey screamed as Jesse pulled her to the ground with him, covering her body with his. Before he'd shielded Casey, he'd seen Tannin's body riddled with bullets.

Had Casey seen, too?

He became aware that he still covered her when he felt her trembling beneath him. Easing away from her, he saw her tear-stained cheeks.

"Shh." With his thumb, he wiped at the moisture. "It's all over now."

She sobbed into his shoulder. Pain at her anguish sliced through him. She'd had to endure the stress of a stalker for months upon months, and now it had culminated in the midst of a dangerous crime-ring takedown.

Casey had known what was happening tonight and she'd purposefully brought her stalker here.

She was one strong woman. He wanted to kiss her, tell her how much he loved her. Convince her this time.

But…not yet.

Timing was everything.

* * *

Casey was completely spent. Drained, she pulled her face from Jesse's wet shirt. On the floor, he cradled her. She felt like a wimp, but she was finally allowing all her buried emotions and frustrations to spill. Finally, he stood and helped her to her feet.

Men wearing shirts and jackets that said police and ICE on them, spoke with Jesse. The men he worked with as an agent, the behind-the-scenes heroes. Yet, for the most part, his attention remained on her.

A dreaded familiar face stepped through the loading-dock doors, hands behind his back. Knife Guy!

Another man guided him, a bloody gash along his forehead. The man shoved Knife Guy toward Jesse, who glanced at Casey.

He motioned for her to join him. "Casey, meet the man responsible for watching you. This is Eric Broderich."

"Ma'am." Eric nodded, barely offering a smile. "I'm sorry I let you down."

"Oh, please don't say that. You're a hero."

Jesse grinned, clearly pleased with the outcome of today's events. "And meet Joseph Tannin, Will's brother. He was dishonorably discharged from the military earlier this year."

Casey took a step back. So, Knife Guy was Will's brother? Had he also been the genius behind the newspaper hacks? Had he given Will Tannin her

cell-phone number? He'd been telling the truth—
he'd known where she was all along because his
brother had followed her and knew she was staying
at her aunt's home.

Eric rubbed the back of his neck. "He owed Will,
and was doing the dirty work for him—even putting you in the freezer, toying with you until tonight, when Will was going to show up and finish
you off."

"This time, he would have killed you," Jesse said,
and took a step toward her. He reached for her hand.
"You did good, leading him here."

She looked at Jesse, whose eyes caressed her with
admiration and something much more.

Love.

If not for him, Will's brother could very well have
done her in already.

Guilt squeezed her chest. Once she'd discovered
his true identity, she hadn't trusted him.

But tonight, she'd seen the real Jesse in action
with her own eyes. He'd left the sting operation to
save her.

Tannin's appearance on the scene had forced her
here tonight. Though she wasn't sure what to expect,
she'd found safety in Jesse's arms. She could trust
him with her life, of that she had no doubt.

And...with my heart.

But would she get the opportunity now?

She gazed up at him. "Thank you for saving me."

God had sent him to protect her. All these months and she thought He had forgotten about her, but He'd been with her all along.

"You're welcome. Are you okay?" Jesse asked.

"Physically, yes." Casey laughed a little.

Eric escorted Joseph Tannin away.

Casey pressed her hand against Jesse's arm. "What about Will?"

By the expression on his face, she knew the answer. Her knees grew weak and she felt herself slipping toward the floor.

Jesse grabbed her, supporting her. "We should get you to the ambulance. It's waiting outside. They can check you over."

What? Wait. "Can I...see him?"

He shook his head. "Casey, you don't want to do that."

After all these months of wishing him out of her life, Casey didn't know how to feel about his death. Yes, she would no longer have to be concerned about him. "But, he's dead. I..."

She what?

"It's a shock, I understand," Jesse said. He ushered her from the warehouse, and she allowed him, her thoughts wrapped around what had happened tonight.

"And what about your friend, Miguel?" Had she just said the word *friend?* Nausea whirled in her stomach.

"Miguel was injured in the gunfire, but he'll be fine. He's on his way to the hospital now."

"Should we go to be with him? Will his wife and child be there?"

Jesse stopped and turned Casey to face him. Again, he cupped her face and spoke in gentle tones. "Miguel is going to be fine. He acted selflessly when helping me with Tannin. He's already providing information to us, and that will garner him a lighter sentence."

Law-enforcement authorities were busy at work around them as blue-and-red lights flashed from their vehicles outside. Casey saw an ambulance waiting at the loading-dock entrance.

"Jesse..."

He pressed a finger against her lips. "There's plenty of time for us to talk. Right now, let's get you checked out. Then I have a surprise for you."

No way was Casey waiting for that. "Surprise? What surprise?"

Jesse laughed for the first time that night. "Your aunt and uncle's flight should be arriving in the next half hour. I thought I'd take you to meet them at the airport."

Casey grew somber. "Thank you, Jesse. I recognize what you did for me tonight. You were willing to blow your cover to save me. I just don't know why."

Jesse's gaze nearly melted her. She wanted him to tell her that he loved her like he'd done before. Was he holding back now because she'd thrown it back in his face?

Please, Lord, no...

"I promise you the full story, if you want it. But first, I think you should know my real name."

Of course, she wanted the real story—any other time in her life she'd be ecstatic to hear those words. But right now, she only wanted to hear three little words. Casey tried to hide her disappointment.

Still, learning his real name was probably the right foundation on which to build a relationship, if they even had a future together. "Well, what is it? Tom or something?"

He grinned. "It's still Jesse—" he jammed his hands in his pockets and glanced at the floor then back at her "—Jesse Mitchell."

"Oh, thank goodness. I couldn't imagine thinking of you as anything other than a Jesse." She smiled and this time, she was the one to stare at the floor, because Jesse might read her thoughts if he were to look in her eyes.

She wanted to roll the name Casey Mitchell around on her tongue just to hear what that would sound like. But so much had happened. Their relationship was built on a cracking foundation. How could it be restored?

A week later, Casey sat on the sofa in the living room, drinking herbal tea with her aunt, who wasn't a coffee person. Her aunt looked very much like Casey's mother, albeit six years younger. Casey had always admired her aunt, and regretted not being able to spend more time with her. If she ended up staying in Southern California, that would all change.

"I need to contact Eddie to see if he'll have me back. I don't suppose he's happy that my stalker story went to the *Orange Crossings Times*."

"Or the ice company–crime ring story."

Casey detected the pain in her aunt's voice. Though Uncle John hadn't been involved, the news had devastated their business for the time being. Her uncle had felt betrayed by the activities that had taken place at his company, right under his nose, as it were.

Aunt Leann set her teacup on the table next to the sofa. "You know, you don't have to go back to Oregon. You could stay here with us."

With Tannin gone, Casey was free to return to her life—to her apartment and friends, and maybe even her job if her previous editor would have her back.

Casey huffed, hating her indecision. It was difficult not to consider it her old life now.

"I think I could convince Danny to keep me here full-time."

"No doubt there. You've shown him you know

how to get a good story." Aunt Leann traced the rim of her teacup with a shiny red nail.

"What I've shown him is my ability to stumble into trouble," Casey said, and laughed.

Her aunt joined her. She laid a hand over Casey's. "Still, getting into trouble is dangerous. You shouldn't make it a habit."

A habit. The word reminded her of how often she'd ended up in Jesse's arms due to her troubles. They had agreed it was becoming a habit. She'd decided he'd become an addiction.

And right now, she was having withdrawal.

The doorbell rang. "I'll get that," her aunt said, then headed to the door.

He'd been swamped after the bust this week, and she'd barely gotten to see him. She'd been subjected to endless questions regarding Will Tannin, which was ironic, considering she'd left Oregon to be free from him. Now it seemed she'd need to leave Southern California for the same reason.

"Come in," Aunt Leann was saying.

Casey focused on the person in the doorway. She recognized the masculine silhouette instantly. Rising from the sofa, she crossed the living room to greet him.

He nodded and glanced at her aunt, who cleared her throat. "I'll leave you two alone," she said.

"No, I didn't mean to interrupt. Maybe Casey

could walk with me on the beach." His gaze was forceful, passionate.

What had he come to say? Casey's insides trembled. "Where's Simon?" Along with his master, she'd missed the loving dog.

"I wanted us to have some privacy."

"Oh, so it's going to be like that, is it?" Casey smiled and led the way to the deck outside. "You're afraid Simon would overhear and tell someone."

"I'm afraid so," he said.

The deep timbre of his voice sent longing through Casey. A breeze had kicked up during the day. Jesse strolled next to her as they walked on the hard, water-drenched sand, avoiding the waves.

When Jesse said nothing, Casey's curiosity began to burn. "How's Miguel?"

Jesse stopped at her words and turned to face the ocean. "I told you that Miguel would be fine. He's recovering in the hospital, and he's cooperating with the authorities."

"Jesse, I couldn't think what else to say. Isn't it all right to ask? He was a friend to you."

"Did you bring him up to remind me of my betrayal?"

Oh, no. This wasn't going at all like she thought. "No."

Now, Jesse faced her. "Good. I was afraid you still held that against me. That you thought I had used you."

What could she say to that? How could he not have used her, given her proximity to the events? And, hadn't she used him, after a fashion? She'd wanted him near for protection. "You were doing your job. I don't blame you for that."

How could she make him understand how much he meant to her?

He grinned. "Come here." He tugged her to him, the way she'd grown to love. He cupped her face then pressed his lips against hers.

Fire stirred in her heart all the way to her belly. She slipped her arms up and slid them around his neck. "Oh, Jesse…" she murmured, her breath hot against his lips.

Jesse intensified the kiss, seeming to draw life from her even as he poured it back in.

How could she live without this man to hold her, kiss her and protect her? His kiss took her far from the beach and left her floating on his passion.

Too soon, he eased back from the intensity, and his lips were soft against hers, once more. In his lingering, she breathed deeply of him, wanting to be carried away again.

Finally, he pressed his forehead against hers, holding her hands in one of his, and the other against the back of her head.

"I love you and never meant to use you. Do you believe that?"

Looking into his eyes, she nodded. "Yes."

"I need to know how you feel."

Didn't he already know? Casey regretted that she'd treated his love so poorly. "I love you," she finally said, the words a breathy whisper. "Oh, Jesse, how I love you."

Her emotions too intense, Casey squeezed her eyes shut.

"Then you belong with me forever, Casey Wilkes. Will you marry me?"

Tears spilled from the corners of her eyes. "Yes, Jesse. Yes!"

He wrapped his arms around her and swung her in circles while she laughed with joy. They fell to the sand, and Jesse planted kisses all over her face.

"You've made me the happiest man on earth."

Suddenly, a morbid thought slammed into Casey's joy.

"What's the matter?" Jesse asked.

She could hardly stand to hear the fear in his voice. "Will you keep working as an undercover agent?" Casey pushed up on her elbow. "Jesse, how can we make this work?"

He rubbed his thumb down her cheek. "Don't worry. I'm transferring out. That was always the plan. Still, I'm not too sure about having a career in law enforcement if you're an investigative reporter."

She played with the sand. "There would be conflict between us."

He rolled her on top of him and planted another

kiss on her. "I'm willing to take the risk if it means we're together. How about you?"

Laughing, she kissed him back, then said, "Mrs. Jesse Mitchell. I've wanted to say that out loud for a long time."

* * * * *

Dear Reader,

Often we find ourselves in a difficult situation and we wonder why. Many times, the answer to that is a simple one—our own choices have taken us on the course to unhappy circumstances. That's exactly what happened to both Casey Wilkes and Jesse Mitchell in *Freezing Point*. Although their choices and the resulting circumstances are different, their paths cross, and they are each given an opportunity to do something different this time, to make better choices.

Casey realizes that digging too deep for a story sent her into hiding. Jesse knows he can't stand by again and watch others be hurt because he's working undercover. We can't change the past, but we can always make different choices for the future.

Thank goodness our God is a God of second chances, or we'd all be in trouble. I love writing stories about characters who learn from their mistakes and grow. After all, if we're not learning and growing, then we're not living. I pray that you look to God to direct your path in all your ways.

I enjoy hearing from my readers. You can contact me through my website at www.Elizabeth Goddard.com and sign up for my newsletter to receive updates.

Elizabeth Goddard

Questions for Discussion

1. Because her life is threatened, Casey travels nearly a thousand miles away, hoping to hide. In a way, she's starting over someplace new. Have you ever wanted to go somewhere far away and start a new life? Or are you happy with the life you're living? Why or why not?

2. Upon arriving in Southern California, Casey makes it a priority to get a job. She needs the money, and she needs to occupy her thoughts to keep herself from obsessing over the man who is after her. Has there been a time in your life when you turned to work to keep you from your thoughts?

3. Casey stays at her aunt and uncle's home on the beach while they're traveling. Other than the people she meets in her job, she doesn't know anyone in town. Do you think in that situation that finding Christian relationships is a first priority? What would you do instead?

4. Jesse is a man of many talents and, as a result, his undercover position as an ice sculptor almost overwhelms him. After being reprimanded on his last assignment, he wants to do the best job he can on this one, so that he can transfer to

another agency with his good reputation intact. Have you ever felt like you failed at something? How did you handle that? Do you think it's important to make amends or to succeed again to restore your image? Why or why not?

5. Since Casey's life was disrupted and she's hiding, she wants to trust God, but isn't sure she can. If God was watching out for her, why is she now on the run? When Jesse enters her life, Casey considers that God might have sent him to protect her. Have you ever doubted that God was there with you? How did you overcome the doubt? Did you eventually see that God is there for you all the time?

6. Casey doesn't tell Jesse about Will Tannin at first. She hasn't been able to prove that Will has done anything, so isn't sure who she can trust. She fears Jesse won't believe her, or worse, that he will think she brought things on herself by digging for a story. Can you relate to her fears? If so, how? Do you think she should have told him sooner? Why or why not?

7. Working as an undercover agent, Jesse struggles with doing his job and leading a Christian life. Let's face it—working undercover is living a lie. Add to that, Jesse has to walk and talk like a criminal—not exactly a Christian example.

How do you feel about this? Do you believe a person can be a Christian and work undercover? Did you empathize with Jesse's ongoing moral dilemma? Do you think he made the right decision to transfer out of undercover work?

8. In her job as an investigative reporter, Casey works to expose wrongdoing, but sometimes that leads to danger, and other times it can lead to hurting others. How do you feel about Casey's career and digging for the truth? What about digging for dirt, or rather, gossip?

9. In working undercover, agents often have to integrate themselves into the lives of criminals, including getting to know their families and children, and even coming to love them, or consider them as close friends. This happened to Jesse with Miguel and his family. How do you feel about this? Do you think Jesse handled the situation appropriately? Were you surprised at Miguel's loyalty?

10. Both Jesse and Casey live life on the edge. In the story, Casey has come close to death several times. In his line of work, Jesse's chances of being injured or killed are very high. They fall in love with each other quickly in the book. Do you think this is because they each realize life is too short to waste? Given their conflicting

careers, do you believe they will have problems? If you could give advice to either of them on the day before the wedding, what would you say?

11. Casey keeps a diary that she believes gives her the ability to process her thoughts and feelings, helping her to keep her priorities in focus. Do you, or have you ever, kept a diary? In what way do you think it helped you the most?

12. When Will threatens to kill Casey, she makes the decision to flee town. If you had to leave your home quickly, what items would you grab? Are these items most important to your survival? Or are they important to your happiness? Why or why not?

13. Miguel was betrayed by someone he considered a brother, yet he continued to be loyal to Jesse. Were you surprised at Miguel's loyalty? Have you ever felt betrayed? How did you react? Do you see things differently now? Would you change your reaction?

14. Jesse's dilemma with his past and the deeds he has committed in keeping with his job have kept him away from God. He believes that he isn't good enough to talk to God, even though his job ultimately leads to good when criminals are arrested. Has there ever been a time in your life

when you felt uncomfortable talking to God, as if you weren't good enough? How did you handle this?

15. Most of the story centers on Jesse's need to complete his assignment while protecting Casey, and yet protecting her could be the very thing that blows his cover and gets them hurt. Still, he can't stand by and watch her get hurt. Have you ever been in a situation where helping someone or doing the right thing could cost you everything? What did you do?

LARGER-PRINT BOOKS!

LARGER-PRINT BOOKS!

**GET 2 FREE
LARGER-PRINT NOVELS
PLUS 2 FREE
MYSTERY GIFTS**

Larger-print novels are now available...

LILPI1B